PENGUIN BOOKS

1746

FRIENDS AT COURT

HENRY CECIL

KU-114-611

FRIENDS AT COURT

HENRY CECIL

PENGUIN BOOKS
IN ASSOCIATION WITH
MICHAEL JOSEPH

Penguin Books Ltd, Harmondsworth, Middlesex
AUSTRALIA: Penguin Books Pty Ltd, 762 Whitehorse Road,
Mitcham, Victoria

—

First published by Michael Joseph 1956
Published in Penguin Books 1962

—

Made and printed in Great Britain
by Hazell Watson & Viney Ltd
Aylesbury and Slough
Set in Intertype Baskerville

This book is sold subject to the condition
that it shall not, by way of trade, be lent,
re-sold, hired out, or otherwise disposed
of without the publisher's consent,
in any form of binding or cover
other than that in which
it is published

CONTENTS

Chapter 1

A QUESTION OF SILK

═══

ROGER THURSBY was counsel for the defendant. The plaintiff was in the witness box. After Roger had cross-examined him for half an hour the judge asked the witness if he would like to sit down.

'Thank you, my Lord,' said the plaintiff, and sat down. But he would have preferred to run out of the Court, down the street, and into his mother's arms, or, at any rate, to someone kind and comforting. Even those who tell the truth in the witness box can have an uncomfortable time there, but the plaintiff had not even a clear conscience to cheer him. He wished he'd never started the action. He'd been warned that there were difficulties. Difficulties! That was a mild word. And now here was one of the ablest counsel at the junior Bar knocking him round the ring till everything was in a haze. If only he could go down for the count. At any rate it would be over then. He asked for a glass of water. That gave him a moment's breathing space – but only a moment, for the obliging usher brought it all too soon.

'He needs something a bit stronger,' said Roger's opponent, in an undertone. And then, as the witness braced himself for the next blow, temporary relief came to him in a manner he had not anticipated. For, just as Roger said:

'Come, Mr Frail, you don't really mean that, do you?' the judge intervened by saying:

'Just one moment, Mr Thursby, please.' The witness wondered if the judge was going to say – as he had said once before – in quiet but ominous tones: 'Mr Frail, I don't think you're doing yourself justice.' But the judge did not say that or anything like it. Instead, he began:

'Mr Leonard Seaforth Jones,' and, before the witness could even start to wonder what Mr Leonard Seaforth Jones

had to do with the case, he went on : 'Her Majesty having
been pleased to appoint you one of her counsel learned in
the law, will you kindly take your place within the Bar.'

Mr Jones, ordinarily very large and even larger in the
regalia of his full-bottomed wig and Q.C.'s ceremonial dress,
prised himself with some little difficulty along the front row
of counsel's seats until he was approximately in the middle
of the row, and bowed low to the judge. He then turned to
his right and bowed to a Q.C. who was standing at that end
of the row, then to another Q.C. at the other end and
finally he turned round and bowed to the junior Bar. He
was just about opposite Roger when he did this, and he and
Roger exchanged winks. Then Mr Jones turned round,
faced the judge, and sat down.

'Do you move, Mr Jones ?' said the judge.

For answer, Mr Jones stood up, bowed again and then
went, still with some difficulty, along the row and out at the
other end, to wait patiently for his colleagues. When they
had all gone through the necessary motions in that Court,
they would all go to the next Court, where the same process would be repeated. And so on.

The witness eventually became aware that his torture was
being interrupted by the final ceremony in the taking of
silk.

'Miss Drusilla Manville, Her Majesty having been pleased
to appoint you one of her counsel learned in the law, will
you kindly take your place within the Bar.' An extremely
pretty woman, who could not have been more than thirty-
five, went through the formalities. As she bowed to Roger,
her full-bottomed wig looking curiously old as it hung
down her young face, he whispered : 'It suits you very well,
if I may say so.'

'Thank you, sir,' she said, as she turned to face the judge
again.

Roger suddenly remembered that his mother was in Court
and would be wondering what on earth was happening. He
scribbled a note, which he sent to her by a junior clerk : 'I'll
tell you all about it afterwards.'

Ten minutes later he rose to resume his cross-examination of the plaintiff. But by this time the unhappy man had regained his composure sufficiently to indicate that he would like his seconds to throw in the towel.

'When they reach the glass-of-water stage,' Roger told one of his pupils later, 'there's at least an even chance that the end is near.'

Roger had been called to the Bar just over twelve years and in that time he had made almost as much progress as it is possible for a junior to make. During the ceremony of taking silk, another of the new Q.C.s, when bowing to Roger, had said :

'You next year?'

Roger shook his head, but not very convincingly, either to the questioner or to himself. He had, in fact, been thinking of applying for silk for some little time. But it was not a decision to be made in a hurry. The work that he had to do as a junior was of several kinds. He did a great deal of paper work, writing opinions and drafting the technical legal documents required in litigation. Then, quite as important, he acted as midwife, wet-nurse and doctor to a delicate baby case until it became strong and healthy, or, almost as often, strangled it at birth, saying a few words of comfort to the parents. 'Much better to tell you now why you won't win than to explain later why you didn't.'

'But are you quite sure, Mr Thursby? You won't mind my saying that our neighbour, who's a lawyer himself, said that he thought we'd be bound to win and it was he who told me to come to you.'

'Well,' Roger had said, 'I can't deny that I think part of his advice was excellent.'

The other side of Roger's practice as a junior was the conduct of cases in Court, when sometimes he would be opposed by a Q.C. and sometimes by another junior. Occasionally, if the case appeared to be an interesting one, his mother came to listen. And so it happened that, for the first time, she saw part of the ceremony of taking silk.

That night, in trying to explain the ceremony to his

mother, Roger also discussed with her his own future. 'Discussed' is perhaps not quite the correct word. Roger had inherited his father's brains. He was devoted to his mother, but devotion could not blind him to the fact that her intelligence was strictly limited. Nevertheless he nearly always talked over his problems with her. He never analysed his reasons for doing this, but there were really two. First, the discussion was often more or less a monologue by Roger and in any event it helped him come to a decision. Secondly, they both liked the feeling that, whatever the problem, it was apparently shared between them.

'You see, mother,' he said, 'a man may do awfully well as a junior because his paper work is first-class and he's good enough, though not spectacular, in Court. If he takes silk, he has to give up his paper work and may be a complete failure as a silk.'

'Well, dear, why not just become a Queen's Counsel and give up this idea of taking silk?'

'Mother, how often have I got to tell you it's the same thing?'

'Then really, dear, I don't know what you're worrying about. If it were something different, you'd have to choose between the two, but, as they're both the same, it can't make any difference, can it, dear? Or have I got something wrong?'

'When you become a Queen's Counsel you have a silk gown, mother. That's why it's called "taking silk". Don't you remember? I really have told you before.'

'I know, dear. I really will try to remember this time.'

The next day Mrs Thursby was talking to a friend. 'My dear,' she said, 'Roger said something to me last night about taking silk.'

'I'm so glad,' said her friend, 'because now you'll be able to tell me what it means.'

'Well,' said Mrs Thursby, with some confidence, 'it means this.' She stopped for a moment. 'This is what it means,' she went on, with slightly less confidence, 'I'll tell you.' Again she stopped.

'I'm able to tell you,' she went on, after a pause, 'because Roger explained it all most carefully to me.'

There was another pause.

'When you're at the Bar,' she continued eventually, but as though she were repeating a lesson she had not quite learned, 'when you're at the Bar either you're a barrister – or you're not.' There was a moment's silence while Mrs Thursby's friend tried hard to look enlightened. 'That doesn't sound quite right,' said Mrs Thursby.

'Well, I did wonder,' said her friend.

'Because,' went on Mrs Thursby, 'if you're at the Bar you *are* a barrister, aren't you? I wonder what Roger meant, because I'm sure he said that, and it sounded so right when he said it.'

'I expect that's because he *is* a barrister,' said her friend. 'They're so convincing even when what they say is wrong.'

'Yes, I know,' said Mrs Thursby, 'but I'm sure Roger wouldn't tell me anything wrong. Just give me a moment, dear. I'm sure it'll come to me.'

Her friend gave her several moments. Suddenly Mrs Thursby's face lit up.

'I remember,' she said, 'there are two kinds of barrister. That's what I meant. When you're at the Bar you're either one kind or the other. D'you see, dear?'

'You mean – like with apples – either Cox's or Blenheims.'

'Oh – no,' said Mrs Thursby. 'There are lots of kinds of apples. More like grapes – either muscats or the others.'

'And which kind is Roger?'

'I'm afraid,' said Mrs Thursby, 'that's what I've forgotten.'

It was perhaps rather too much for Mrs Thursby to remember that barristers are divided into juniors and Queen's Counsel, and that, as a general rule, the work of a Queen's Counsel is mostly confined to appearing in Court. Roger had explained to her years before, in fact soon after he was called, that being a junior did not necessarily mean that you were young or inexperienced. 'Some of the juniors in the Chancery Division have beards, mother,' he had told her.

'Your father had a beard once, Roger,' his mother had replied. 'I'll find the photograph.'

'And some juniors become judges without ever taking silk, you know,' Roger had continued, while his mother was searching in a drawer.

'Here it is,' she had said a moment later. 'It was red – until he shaved it off – but, of course, the colour doesn't show there.'

About nine months after he had talked about silk to his mother, Roger talked very seriously to his clerk on the subject. Donald Pirbright had been his clerk for over eleven years. Roger had served his year's pupillage with a Mr Grimes and had then gone to other chambers. The clerk in the new chambers was Donald and, during the eleven years, there had grown up between Roger and his clerk the usual indefinable but close relationship which exists between a barrister and his clerk. Donald was an excellent clerk and, like all excellent clerks, he had his idiosyncrasies; they are not called faults in the Temple. When Roger arrived at his chambers in the morning, Donald would call him 'sir.' In the afternoon, after a visit or two to one of his favourite haunts, he would be more likely to say 'sir, sir,' or even 'sir, sir, sir,' and by the evening, as often as not, he called him 'Roger.' The discussion about silk was in the late afternoon.

'Well,' said Roger, 'what about it? Do I or don't I?'

'Next year,' said Donald.

'What's the point of waiting? Bullet and Angel are applying.'

'Sir, sir. Please don't mention Mr Bullet and Mr Angel. Not in the same breath as yourself, sir. Sir, really. Bullet and Angel. Sir, sir, sir.'

'Bullet's not at all bad,' said Roger.

'Bullet,' said Donald, '*Mr* Bullet, I beg his pardon, is bloody hopeless.'

'Anyway, he'll get it.'

'Sir, sir sir, don't come that one on me. Of course he'll get it. He's an M.P. They get it automatically.'

'But why should I wait, anyway?' asked Roger. 'What's the advantage of waiting? Or are you frightened?'

'Now, sir,' said Donald, as sternly as his recent visits to The Feathers would allow, 'now, sir, my clerk's fees don't mean a thing. You know that. I'm surprised at you, sir. I really am.'

Every time that Roger received a fee his clerk received one too. It is not certain who invented the practice, but Roger had thought more than once that there should be a statue in the Temple to the man who had thought of the brilliant idea which resulted in a barrister's clerk being paid not by his employer but by the client. The clerks might perhaps subscribe to a second statue, nestling under the shadow of the first, to the band of heroes among the clerks who, after the 1939–45 war, successfully established the practice by which a barrister pays the shillings in his guineas to the clerk. The idea was not a new one, but it was only after the war that there was a concerted attack on the Bar by the clerks, who, without a shot fired, achieved their object. When barristers and clerks were reunited after the war they naturally discussed their respective adventures during the war and then, as it were by a prearranged signal, in every set of chambers the clerk would say in an almost off-hand way :

'Oh, by the way, sir, we now have the shillings in the guineas.'

A pause.

'That all right with you, sir? They're all doing it, sir.'

Victory was complete almost immediately. A few waverers wandered uncertainly and self-consciously about the Temple for a week or two, but they soon felt that they were being regarded as outcasts and within a very short time :

'Oh, Bernard, I've been thinking about the matter you mentioned the other day.'

'Matter, sir, matter?'

'You know – the shillings in the guineas.'

'Oh – that, sir.'

A pause.

'Well, sir?'

'All right, Bernard, I give in.'

'Thank you very much, sir. They're all doing it, really, sir.'
And they all were. And are.

When Donald said that his clerk's fees didn't mean a
thing, he really meant it. Naturally he would have been
sorry for himself as well as for Roger if, when he took silk,
his practice declined and with it the clerk's fees and the
shillings. But thoughts of that possibility were not uppermost
in his mind and he was thinking almost entirely of Roger's
interests.

'Well, why on earth d'you want me to wait, then? I'm
working sixteen hours a day, week-ends included. I don't
get time for a thing. I've about had enough. I haven't even
had time to get married.'

'Sir, sir, sir,' said Donald. 'That's nothing to do with time.
Find the lady and you'll find the time.'

'But I haven't time to find the lady. If I'm working for
you all night and all day, how can I? No, really, Donald,
it's not good enough. And anyway, you still haven't said
what there is to wait for. I'm making ten thousand a year.
If you think I won't get on as a silk at all, for Heaven's sake
say so. I shan't take any notice, but do say so.'

'Get on, sir, get on? Of course, you'll get on. I'll tell you
something else, sir. You won't be a silk for more than five or
six years – that's if you want to go up. I'm not sure if I'd
come with you myself if you go on the Bench. We'd have to
ask Henry – Mr Blagrove.'

Henry Blagrove was the head of Roger's chambers. He
was seven or eight years older than Roger and was as in-
dolent by nature as Roger was energetic. But his charming
and determined wife, Sally, had spurred him into a little
more activity and he had eventually taken silk. He was extremely able and, as a silk, he had just about the size practice he wanted. Sally was a solicitor, but she had given up
practice to have babies and Roger was godfather of their first.
Theirs was a very happy set of chambers. If Roger became
a High Court judge, Donald could have gone with him as

clerk or stayed with Henry, and it was a difficult choice to make. However, that was a long way ahead at the moment.

'Well, if I'm going to get on as a silk, why not now? Tell me that.'

'All right, sir, if that's how you want it – now it shall be. All the same, I'd have liked to have seen another year's junior work behind you.'

'You wouldn't have to do it, Donald,' said Roger. 'You can play golf and take your wife out, while I sit sweating at home. Now we'll reverse the process. I can sit twiddling my thumbs while you search the highways and by-ways to find me a brief.'

'Search the highways, my foot,' said Donald.

'That's really all I wanted to know,' said Roger. 'P'raps you'd turn up the Law List and tell me all the people I've got to write to. How many d'you think there'll be?'

Roger now had the task of writing to every practising junior on his circuit, who was senior to him in call, to inform him of his intention to apply to the Lord Chancellor for the purpose of taking silk, so that they could apply also if they wanted to do so. It was a task to which he looked forward. It meant that he had made up his mind. It was a risk un-doubtedly, but it was worth it. The only question now was whether the Lord Chancellor would give it him first time. He was certainly young – thirty-three – but there was no doubt about the size and quality of his practice. He did not think that he would receive – as some promising juniors had received in the past – a polite note with 'next time' on it. Anyway, if he did, the decision would have been made for him. That night he wrote a letter to the Permanent Secre-tary to the Lord Chancellor :

I shall be grateful if you will place before the Lord Chancellor this my application to be considered for appointment as one of Her Majesty's Counsel.

He showed it to his mother.

'How many Q.C.s are there, dear?' she asked.

'I don't know – altogether, I suppose, about three to four

hundred, but I should say that only about half of them practise.'

'The Queen must have a lot of cases to need all those counsel.'

Roger did his best to explain.

'You make it all sound very clear,' said his mother.

'Good,' said Roger.

'But I'm afraid,' she went on, 'I still don't understand. All the same, I'm glad you'll be one of them. But don't ask her too many questions.'

Some little time was to elapse before the Lord Chancellor's decision would be known and meantime Roger carried on with his ordinary work. But he did so in a much happier frame of mind. He could see the way ahead and there would be some time in it for other things besides law. He was very cheerful when he lunched next day at the Inn he used for the purpose. He usually sat with the same people, though he could never quite think why. Probably it was habit. They had been his neighbours when he first lunched in that Hall some years ago before and it seemed rude to sit elsewhere. In any event, lunch did not take long. The conversation during it was usually on the same lines. Arnold Carruthers, who sat opposite him, was a barrister of a good many years' experience. He found it helped him to discuss his professional problems with other people and almost invariably he would begin, as soon as he decently could – and sometimes before :

'Look, I'm an actress of uncertain age and not much talent. I get knocked down by a bus. What's it worth? I couldn't act much before the accident. Can't act at all now.'

Sometimes it would be a point of law. 'Look, the Court of Appeal in *Lea and Moore* seem to have said that you can't try a case in the County Court by consent unless it first started in the High Court. I'm referring, of course, to cases which are outside the normal jurisdiction. But they only looked at Section 43. They never once referred to Section 65. Now, I think –' And Carruthers would elaborate his point and try to obtain the opinions of those around him. If he was lucky someone would point out that a new Act did away with the effect of the decision.

Another of Roger's neighbours had a very small practice, a reasonable private income, and a fund of undergraduate stories. He began on this occasion with : 'D'you know this one? There was a girl with a rather short skirt standing in a bus. The conductor gave her a ticket, but she dropped it. "Will it matter?" she asked the conductor. Have you heard it by the way?'

'Only once or twice,' said his immediate neighbour, 'and not for a very long time.'

'Well, I don't suppose Thursby knows it. He's never heard any of them.'

'No, I haven't, as a matter of fact,' said Roger politely, 'but it'll probably be above my head.'

'Oh, no – not this one. Well – the conductor turned to the girl and said –'

At that moment Carruthers arrived.

'Look, so sorry to butt in, but I've got rather a teaser. D'you mind? I'm a stable boy at a well-known racing stable –'

'Got anything for the Derby?'

'No, look, this is serious –'

'Then the girl said : "But how shall I know if it's the right ticket?" Then the conductor turned to the girl and said –'

'And while I'm out exercising a horse which I haven't ridden before –'

'Hullo, Roger, they tell me you're applying for silk.'

'But I've only just posted the letter –'

'Good news travels fast.'

'Then the girl turned to a passenger and said : "I wonder if you'd mind –" '

'Now this horse was well known to the trainer to be difficult, but I didn't know it. Now, while I'm on this brute –'

'Good news! If I get it first time, I expect I'll be in the bread line.'

'Rubbish – I hear Forsythe's applied.'

'Is there anything confidential you don't know?'

'Confidential be blowed. I bet you've written to at least thirty people on your circuit.'

'More, if you want to know.'

'Well, you can't expect them all to keep quiet about it.'

'Then the girl said –'

'As I fell on the ground the trainer arrived and cursed me. What he actually said was –'

And so on and so forth, what the girl said, how the conductor turned, why the stable boy fell, what the trainer called him, interspersed with the latest gossip and a few polite inquiries. And lunch in Hall was over.

Chapter 2

RETROSPECT

———

THAT evening Roger walked home from chambers. He thought first about the past, about his call nearly thirteen years before, his first miserable efforts in Court, the agonies he had gone through. How kind Henry Blagrove had been. He was sure he would never have got on but for Henry. It was not simply the encouragement Henry had given him, but he had shown him the only way to learn how to succeed at the Bar. I wonder if I've taught my pupils half as much as Henry taught me? Never accept anything without knowing why, Henry had always told him. Whether it's a matter of law or practice, you must know the principle behind it. When the judge says : 'But you can't do that,' find out why you can't do it, and very occasionally, in looking up to see why you can't do it, you'll find you can and that the judge was wrong. Yes, he owed nearly everything to Henry. He was glad that Henry owed something to him too – Sally. Roger found it difficult to remember himself and his girl friends without squirming. Who, outside of Dornford Yates, would have behaved as I did – or, indeed, as they did? Sally and Joy had both adored Roger. Roger at twenty-one, good-looking, ambitious, slightly priggish, wholly inexperienced was, to Roger at thirty-three, a somewhat nauseating spectacle. But he braced himself to the effort of looking back. And after all he had been very young. He thought of Joy, pretty and empty-headed. Well, perhaps not as empty as all that. She had sent her uncle to brief him, Uncle Alfred, that pompous elderly solicitor whom he had eventually insulted by refusing a three-thousand-guinea brief. How on earth had I the nerve? Three thousand guineas and we were very short of money at the time. But it would have meant marrying Joy. How right he had been. And as for Sally, who had more intelligence than any woman he had ever known, Sally adoring, rather lovely and rather sad. I wonder why I never wanted to marry her? I suppose because I just didn't want to marry at all. Anyway, my loss, if it was one, was Henry's gain. He fell for Sally and eventually she capitulated. They were very happy. I am pleased about that, he thought. If it hadn't been for me, Henry would never have met her. That's something I've done for him. All the same, I could do with a home now. I wonder if I'll get one. I'll certainly get more spare time soon, at least I hope so. Well, I'm not going to waste it. Why on earth do I lunch with Carruthers and Co.? I joined Henry's Inn in addition to my own and I have to go and listen to that tripe. There were plenty of other people in Hall who seldom talked shop and never told dirty stories. I can't very well move somewhere else when I take silk. Oh – well I suppose I'm used to it by now. But that girl in the bus went on for ever. I don't even remember the end now. Perhaps I never heard it. I expect it was as old as the hills, anyway. His stories aren't just chestnuts – more like *marrons glacés*. Anyway, what am I worrying about? I'm going to take silk, marry and have a home. Life begins at thirty-three.

Chapter 3

SLOGRAVE, PLUMB AND CO.

===

'So Donald's letting you apply,' said Henry the next day. 'That's very decent of him. Of course, it'll ruin me, but don't let that worry you.'

'If I get any of your leavings, I shall be lucky,' said Roger.

'Leavings? I haven't returned a brief this year, but don't let it get you down. As a matter of fact, I'll exist quite well on *your* returns. You wait and see.'

'I haven't got silk yet.'

'You will. It's a foregone conclusion with your practice. Donald's a very lucky man. All he wants now is a junior who can take on your practice. D'you think Axford will hold it?'

Axford was older than Roger, but had not been in the chambers as long. He had started as a solicitor and then read for the Bar.

'I think he ought to keep some of it. He's a good lawyer and works like a black.'

At that moment Donald came into the room. 'Slograve, Plumb have just been on the phone. Want to come and see you at once. I said O.K.'

'All right,' said Roger. 'Any excuse for not getting on with some work.'

'It was Plumb himself. He sounded rather worried.'

'He's always gloomy. When you start a case he's worried to death that the witnesses won't come up to scratch and, if they do, that the judge won't. Then, if you win the case, he's terrified it'll go to the Court of Appeal and, if you win there, he has sleepless nights thinking of the House of Lords allowing the appeal. Then, when the Lords dismiss the appeal with costs, he's on tenterhooks that the other side won't have the money to pay. And when they've paid in full, he's pretty sure to point out that the amount he's had to charge his client is more than they've got out of the other side. And if you point out to him that he could have charged a bit less, that worries him more than anything – because it happens to be true.'

'I like your Mr Plumb,' said Henry. 'There's a richness about his gloom which I enjoy. One can almost pinch it as Mr Squeers pinched young Wackford. "There's oiliness for you." Don't forget me if they want a leader, Donald. Oh – by the way, I backed your confounded horse on Saturday.'

Donald owned two racehorses. He called one 'Conference' and the other 'Consultation'. He had bought them from a trainer for whom Roger had done a case.

'I didn't tell you to, sir. If you want to win on my horses, you wait till I give the word.'

'Sally and I are going to Alexandra Park on Saturday. Have you got anything for us?'

'I'll come back and see you when I've seen Mr Plumb in, sir. Conference is coughing at the moment. Consultation looks extremely well. The only trouble with that horse is that it doesn't like jockeys. Once it's thrown its jockey it goes like the wind. Almost flies you might say. I thought of suggesting to the Jockey Club they might try some riderless races. Have some corn beyond the winning-post. That'd stop them. Oh – there's the bell. I expect that's old Plumb. Excuse me, sir.'

'I'll go to my room,' said Roger.

A few minutes later Mr Plumb was shown in to him. He had a red face and a bald head, and whether it was hot or not he was continually wiping it with a handkerchief. He sat down rather ponderously, wiped imaginary sweat from his forehead, sighed, frowned and then spoke. He had a voice reminiscent of that of the Radio Doctor but lacking its cheerfulness.

'It's very lucky indeed,' he said in the gloomiest possible tones, 'very lucky indeed you're not in Court, Mr Thursby. It's a great relief.' He wiped his forehead again. 'I don't know what I should have done. There's no one else in the Temple I could go to.'

'It's very good of you to say so,' said Roger, 'but I'm sure there is.'

'But there isn't, Mr Thursby, there really isn't. That's what's so worrying. You may take silk one day and then where shall we be?'

'And, of course, I might be knocked down by a bus,' said Roger gently.

Mr Plumb said nothing.

'Well – I'll take all the care of myself I can,' said Roger. 'And we'll hope for the best.'

'Mr Thursby,' began Mr Plumb, and then stopped.

'Yes?' said Roger.

Mr Plumb hesitated.

'Well,' said Roger cheerfully, 'what's it all about?'

Mr Plumb again hesitated. He appeared to be in two minds as to what he wanted to say. Eventually one of his minds forged ahead, and he spoke :

'Well, Mr Thursby, I act for the proprietors of a seaside hotel. The Glorious at Westlea. It's a most respectable place, I assure you, terribly respectable. I've known Mr and Mrs Glacier – they own the place – for many years. They are very good clients, very good clients indeed.' As he said this, Mr Plumb looked so mournful that Roger really wondered whether he was going to burst into tears.

'They buy hotels all over the place and, I may tell you in confidence, the conveyancing is worth a very considerable sum, a very considerable sum indeed.'

Mr Plumb looked gloomier than ever.

'And what's happened? Have they stopped conveying?'

Mr Plumb wiped his forehead and was silent for a moment. Then his other mind came to the front and took command.

'Mr Thursby,' he said, 'my firm briefs you because I believe you to be without question easily the best junior at the Common Law Bar. I hope you will forgive my speaking plainly.'

'No one could object to such plainness, however undeserved,' said Roger.

'The plainness is to come, Mr Thursby. Because of our opinion of you, my partner and I accept your little bouts of facetiousness with as much goodwill as we can muster. But neither of us has much of a sense of humour, Mr Thursby. I know it is not fashionable to say so, but we have not. We are gloomy men, Mr Thursby, gloomy men.'

'I'm so sorry,' murmured Roger.

'Thank you,' said Mr Plumb, 'and would I be out of order if I asked you to add to your many kindnesses by not laughing at me too obviously too often? I'm consulting you about a most serious matter, very serious indeed, and while I shall quite understand if in the circumstances you ask me to leave your chambers, if you do not take that course I shall be grateful if you will at any rate conceal your amusement. No doubt sometimes you may indulge in a quip which, owing to my lack of humour, will go over my head and out of the window and maybe will rocket into the satellites. Pray do so, if you wish, so long as you are reasonably certain I shall not notice it.'

'I'm so sorry,' said Roger. 'I really am. Please don't take any notice of my flippancy. I apologize for it. It's very rude. I must confess, though, that, however serious a case, a light touch every now and then helps things along. I have even heard a judge make a joke in sending a man to prison.'

'And may I ask,' said Mr Plumb, 'did it send the fellow roaring with laughter to the cells?'

'A fair comment, Mr Plumb, and not one I should expect from anyone without a sense of humour. I think, if I may say so, you have one somewhere around.'

'It is of course possible,' said Mr Plumb with the utmost gloom. 'It is of course possible.' And he wiped his forehead.

'But to continue about my clients,' he went on. 'Mr and Mrs Glacier are Swiss by birth, but they are naturalized. They have lived here a considerable time. They started with very little capital and have worked up a magnificent business – magnificent. It is all very depressing.'

Roger restrained himself from asking what was depressing about that.

'Mr Thursby, solicitors have their feelings. I know that people are inclined to regard lawyers as soulless bloodsuckers – but Slograve, Plumb are at any rate not without a soul.'

A little rhyme insisted on inserting itself in Roger's thoughts

> High-minded but dumb
> Slograve, Plumb

but he kept it to himself.

'I won't deny,' continued Mr Plumb, 'that the loss of their business would not mean a lot to us. It would. A very great deal.'

I convey, you convey, he conveys, went through Roger's mind.

'Indeed, such a loss could be a very serious blow to our business.'

Would that I may convey, would that you may convey, would that they (and in particular Mr and Mrs Glacier) may convey. May they convey, let them convey – consult Roger Thursby and they *shall* convey.

'But at the moment I am thinking not so much of our firm as of these two people. A man and a woman. My clients.'

Meet to be conveyed, considered Roger.

'Ruin, Mr Thursby. A life's work gone. Gaol. Naturalization cancelled. Back to Switzerland.'

How will they be conveyed? resisted Roger. Instead: 'How does it all arise?' he asked.

'It's absurd really,' said Mr Plumb, 'quite absurd. But, like so many serious matters, it arises from a small one. The licensing laws. The requirements with which licensees have to comply are very considerable and sometimes onerous, very onerous indeed. For example, there is no objection to a licensee giving a friend a drink after hours if he chooses. But who is a friend?'

'Who is my neighbour?' asked Roger.

'Precisely. An equally difficult question. A landlord of a hotel should be a friend to his guests.'

'It's a prosecution for a breach of the licensing laws?' queried Roger.

'If that were all,' said Mr Plumb, 'I should not have troubled you with the matter. That would be serious, but nothing more. It is far worse than that.'

He wiped his forehead several times. Roger was tempted to ask him if he would like a glass of water, but he refrained.

'You can imagine the shock it was to me when my clients came to me only this morning – you'll see I've wasted no time in coming to you – when they came to me and said they had been charged with bribery of the police. Bribery of the police. A conviction for that and they're finished in this country, apart from the fact that they'd probably go to prison. Mr Thursby, I don't ask you to take my word for it, but Mr and Mrs Glacier are charming and respectable people.'

And require a lot of conveyancing, added Roger to himself.

'I cannot for one moment think them guilty, but there it is, they're charged – under the Prevention of Corruption Act. Now, I believe in acting under counsel's advice from the word go – not, I may say, because that relieves us of legal responsibility, but because – provided you go to the right counsel – it pays – it pays us, it pays the client.'

And the client pays counsel, said Roger – again to himself. But he knew Mr Plumb was right. And, indeed, he encouraged his clients to come to him at an early stage. Many an action has been won or lost by the preliminary steps which have been taken long before it ever came into Court.

'Now I might have gone to Mr Erswell of the Criminal Bar – a very sound man, if I may say so. But I wanted something better than that. Erswell is, if I may say so, excellent in Court, admirable at putting his case – when it's been prepared for him in an adequate brief – before judge or jury. But I have a feeling that this matter requires rather more imagination in its handling. So I've come to you and I hope – I earnestly hope you'll be able to help us.'

'I'll certainly do my best, Mr Plumb,' said Roger. 'Perhaps you'll tell me the facts.'

'I'd prefer to call them allegations, Mr Thursby. They are these. There have been rather late parties at the Glorious from time to time and apparently neighbours objected to the noise. I need hardly say that the parties were entirely respectable, but admittedly they were late and admittedly you cannot have a party without a noise. Apparently complaints were made to the police and, in consequence, somehow or other plain-clothes detectives attended one or two occasions. A few weeks ago an inspector and a sergeant from the local police station called on Mr and Mrs Glacier and informed them that they would be proceeded against for breach of the licensing laws. It is alleged that at that interview and again at a subsequent interview Mr and Mrs Glacier attempted to bribe the officers by handing them, on the first occasion, twenty pounds in one-pound notes and, on the second occasion, twenty-five pounds. It is alleged that the money was handed to the police to persuade them either to stop the prosecution or to make the offence appear to be a very trivial one.'

'I can understand your anxiety, Mr Plumb,' said Roger. 'What do your clients say about it? Do they admit giving the money?'

'Most certainly not,' said Mr Plumb. 'And I may tell you, Mr Thursby, that I believe them.'

'Well,' said Roger, 'I haven't met either of them and I haven't yet heard them tell their story, but I'll tell you quite frankly I shall be very surprised if their story is true. Now, please don't get excited, Mr Plumb.'

For Mr Plumb had started to brush his forehead very vigorously indeed.

'I'm not in the least excited,' said Mr Plumb, his red face redder and his handkerchief doing overtime. 'I'm not in the least excited, but am I to understand that you are calling my clients liars?'

'Certainly not,' said Roger, 'not yet. I tell you, I haven't seen them or heard them tell their story. Of course, I can't form a judgement on them yet. But just consider what it means if they're telling the truth. It means that an inspector and a sergeant – with very likely as many years of good character behind them as your clients – have put their heads together for no known reason to pretend that they have received money from your clients.'

'You're not suggesting, Mr Thursby, that the police never tell lies and never trump up cases?'

'No,' said Roger. 'It does happen occasionally, but there has to be a reason for it. And don't forget this. Those pound notes – forty-five of them, I think you said, are going to be produced at the trial. And I'll tell you who'll produce them.'

'The inspector and the sergeant, I presume?'

'Certainly not. Possibly even the local Chief Constable, and at least the Superintendent. After your clients handed these notes to the police officers – I mean after they *didn't* hand them to the police officers, these police officers on two separate occasions handed two separate bundles of notes to a superior officer. Now, of course, the Superintendent or the Chief Constable might be in the swindle, but I imagine you'll agree that that's going a bit far. So that, apparently, just in order to do down your clients, the inspector and sergeant laid their hands on forty-five pound notes and took them to the Superintendent or some superior officer, with a fraudulent story that your clients had tried to bribe them. Now it's one thing to invent a story. It's another to invent forty-five pound notes. They have to be obtained and they were obtained. Quite a lot of money, you know, for police officers to have. Much too dangerous to have drawn them from a bank or the post office. They must have kept them under the bed.'

The movement of Mr Plumb's hand had slowed down a bit.

'Mr Thursby,' he said, 'you shake me. But I still can't believe it. I'm sure there's some explanation.'

'I think perhaps,' said Roger, 'you'd better bring your clients to see me and we'll hear what it is. I'm in Court all day tomorrow, but I expect Donald can fix a conference after 4.30.'

Chapter 4

MR GRIMES

═══

ROGER was in Court the next day dealing with a contract for the supply of machinery to Peru. The case was expected to last a long time. His opponent was Mr Grimes. The judge was Mr Justice Chance.

'How are ye, my dear fellow?' said Mr Grimes to Roger outside the Court. 'A little bird tells me ye've applied for silk. Good for you, my dear fellow, good for you. But –' and Mr Grimes shook his head, 'things aren't what they used to be, my dear fellow, not what they used to be. Ye'll find it a bit of a teaser, my dear fellow. Silks are two a penny, my dear chap, two a penny.'

'I'm going to charge twopence,' said Roger.

'That's the way, my dear fellow, that's the way, but I don't know what we're coming to. D'ye know, I've had a dozen letters from fellows on my circuit – they were only called yesterday – I don't know what they think will happen to them, but there it is, my dear fellow, they will do these things, they will do these things. Now, what about this case of ours, my dear fellow, my clients aren't at all inclined to settle it, ye know.'

'Nor are mine,' said Roger.

'Stubborn, my dear fellow, stubborn,' said Mr Grimes.

'It's dogged as does it,' said Roger.

'I beg your pardon?' said Mr Grimes.

'Nothing,' said Roger. 'But why should you want to settle? You've an unanswerable case and a hopeless opponent. What more could anyone want?'

'I can't understand your chaps fighting it, my dear fellow, I really can't,' said Mr Grimes.

'Nor can I,' said Roger. 'But it's lucky some of them will.

Between you and me they're only doing it to keep me in practice.'

'Ye will pull my leg, my dear fellow, ye will pull my leg,' said Mr Grimes. 'But all the same, my dear fellow, I think ye'd be wise to make me an offer. I think ye'd be wise.'

'If you'd said that twelve years ago I should have put my head on the block and invited you to chop it off.'

'Was it as much as twelve years ago, my dear fellow, was it really?'

'Well, you haven't changed. As young and bustling as ever. What's your record from the Temple to the Bear Garden?'

Mr Grimes never walked if he could trot and never trotted if he could run. Age had slowed him down a little, but only a little. The policemen on duty outside the Law Courts seldom needed to hold up the traffic for Mr Grimes; he was across the Strand almost before they'd seen him. It would have been an exceptionally skilled motorist who could have caught him. But he always complained bitterly : 'When they've killed a judge, my dear fellow,' he used to say, 'they'll put a bridge up or a subway. Till then one just has to take a chance. Good-bye, my dear fellow, so nice to have seen ye – good-bye, bye, bye.'

The 'byes' floated across the Strand as Mr Grimes dodged a bus, slipped behind a lorry, glared at a cyclist and cannoned into a pedestrian on the other side. 'So sorry, my dear fellow, it's these –' but by this time he was up the stairs leading to the Bear Garden and the pedestrian never learned what 'these' were.

'Oh, I don't know,' said Mr Grimes to Roger, 'one can't quite do what one used to do, you know, one can't quite do it.'

'Well, you seem to,' said Roger. 'I don't notice the slightest difference.'

'That's very kind of ye, my dear fellow, very kind of ye. Now, what about this case? Ye really ought to make an offer.'

'I said you hadn't changed,' said Roger. 'No, I think we'll see what old Chance thinks of the preliminary point. If he's against us on it, I might offer you something. Not much, mind you.'

'That's all right, my dear fellow, my people don't want to settle. Ye have a fight, my dear fellow, and see where it gets ye.'

As Roger said nothing and was about to go into Court, Mr Grimes added : 'Why don't ye offer something, my dear fellow?'

'You seem in a bad way,' said Roger. 'Let's see. You're claiming five thousand pounds. I'll offer you two hundred and fifty.'

'Two hundred and fifty pounds, my dear fellow, two hundred and fifty pounds?' Mr Grimes almost screamed. 'That won't even pay the costs.'

'I don't suppose it will,' said Roger, 'but it'll be something towards them.'

'If that's all ye've got to say,' said Mr Grimes, 'we'd better go into Court.'

'I was just going,' said Roger, 'when you stopped me.'

'Why not make it one thousand pounds, my dear fellow? I might persuade my people to take it.'

'I'll make it guineas,' said Roger.

'A thousand guineas?'

'Oh – no . . . two-fifty.'

'It's ridiculous, my dear fellow. I tell ye it will only just pay the brief fee.'

'That'd be something.'

'The judge'll be coming in, my dear fellow, shall we ask him to stay out for a bit?'

'All right,' said Roger, who recognized the white flag when he saw it. He called for Donald.

'See if you can keep the judge back for a bit. It looks as though this is going to be settled.'

'I'll try, sir,' said Donald, 'but you know what this judge is like.'

Roger did know, and so did everyone else. Chance J. had a sweet smile and a melodious voice. He never raised it, he seldom said a harsh word to anyone. It is said that on one occasion he smiled so pleasantly at the prisoner he was about to sentence that the poor fellow couldn't believe it when he got ten years. He even appealed on the ground that it must have been a mistake. Chance J. always sat at 10.30 a.m. He had done it for years and proposed to go on doing so. He expected everyone else to do the same. He expected every case to be ready at the appointed time. If counsel was late he found his case struck out or at least put to the bottom of the list. And what made it worse, Chance J. was so nice about it.

'A traffic accident, Mr Peabody?' he had been known to say. 'I'm so very sorry. It must have been very difficult for you. No doubt you'll come by train next time. Much more reliable. I've had your case put to the bottom of the list. I doubt whether it will be heard today. I'm so very sorry. Please explain the matter to your client. I'm sure he'll understand. Yes, Mr Blank, I'll take your application for an adjournment now. It is refused. Thank you so much.'

However, Donald went hastily off to find Mr Justice Chance's clerk. They were old friends, played cricket together and had stood each other drinks at every bar within three hundred yards of the Law Courts.

'Hello, old boy, what can I do for you?'

'Keep the old — back for a bit.' The — was in fact unspoken. That was out of respect for the Bench. You just looked the word, gave a momentary pause and the decencies were observed.

'Have a heart,' said the judge's clerk. 'I couldn't even keep him back for the Attorney. "I'll start the next case," he said when I asked him. "There isn't one," I said. "This is supposed to take all day." "Well, go and draw one from someone else. I'm sitting at 10.30."'

'Doesn't he ever remember he was at the Bar?'

'Now you've said something. Between you and me, I told him myself. "James," he said, "I used to wait hours when I was at the Bar. I didn't like it, but I had to. Now I'm not going to wait any more." But he said it all so nicely there was nothing I could say. Really, I daren't ask him, old boy. I'd do it for you if I'd do it for anyone. It'd be no good if I did. He'd simply give me a sweet smile. "Shall we go in, James?" he'd say.'

So at 10.30 a.m. precisely Roger's and Mr Grimes's case was duly called on immediately after Mr Justice Chance had taken his seat. Mr Grimes was whispering furiously to his clients, as the associate said :

'*Green, Rawhide, and Smithers* against *Confucios.*'

Mr Grimes rose : 'I wonder whether your Lordship would grant me a few minutes' indulgence?'

The judge smiled sweetly. 'Indulgence, Mr Grimes?' he said most amiably.

'Just a few minutes, me Lud. Your Ludship may not be troubled with the case.'

'But it's no trouble, Mr Grimes. That's what I'm here for.'

'But, me Lud,' began Mr Grimes unhappily.

'That's all right, Mr Grimes,' said the judge. 'Pray open the case. It has a South American flavour, if one may judge from the defendants' name. Oil, Mr Grimes?'

'Machinery, me Lud.'

'Ah, machinery. You'll have to treat me very gently, Mr Grimes. Nice simple language, please. Is there a model in Court? I see something down there which –'

The judge put on his glasses.

'Oh – no, I'm sorry,' he added.

It was Mr Grimes's client.

'Now, I think we've wasted enough time, Mr Grimes. Shall we get on?' and he gave Mr Grimes the kind of beaming smile he had given the prisoner who had got the ten years. 'Now, please, Mr Grimes,' he went on without the slightest show of irritation – indeed still smiling – as Mr Grimes turned round and started murmuring feverishly to his client. 'Please, Mr Grimes, conferences afterwards. At one o'clock, shall we say?'

'I'll take five hundred pounds,' whispered Mr Grimes to Roger.

'Sorry,' said Roger. 'Two-fifty.'

'Guineas,' said Mr Grimes.

'Certainly,' said Roger.

'Mr Grimes,' said the judge, 'can you hear me?'

'Oh, me Lud, I beg your Ludship's pardon, but I'm glad to tell your Ludship that your Ludship will not be troubled – that me learned friend and I have come to terms.'

'A close thing, Mr Grimes,' said the judge. 'Do you want any order from me?'

'I suggest, my Lord,' said Roger, 'that the action should be stayed on terms endorsed on counsel's brief.'

'I think I should have a judgment, me Lud,' said Mr Grimes.

'Dear, dear,' said the judge. 'I thought I was told that the parties had come to terms. Either they have or they haven't. That's right, isn't it, Mr Grimes?'

'Oh – yes, me Lud.'

'Mr Thursby?'

'Certainly, my Lord.'

'I'm so glad we're agreed,' said the judge. 'Now, perhaps Mr Grimes would kindly open the case or tell me the agreed terms.'

'Won't you agree to a judgment, my dear fellow,' whispered Mr Grimes to Roger.

'I don't mind,' said Roger.

A few minutes later Mr Justice Chance started the hearing of the next case, and Roger and Mr Grimes left the Court.

'Tell me,' said Roger when they were outside, 'why did you crack like that? You hadn't such a bad case.'

'Ye're quite right, my dear fellow, I *hadn't* such a bad case at all – yesterday. But that agent fellow suddenly turned round and went back on his proof. So what could I do, my dear fellow, but still there it is, my dear fellow, they will do these things.'

Chapter 5

MR AND MRS GLACIER

WITH a long case out of the way, Roger was able to go back to chambers, and Mr Plumb was informed that he could have an earlier conference if he wished it. He jumped at the opportunity and telephoned his clients, Mr and Mrs Glacier, to meet him at Roger's chambers. They all arrived just before 3 p.m. and Mr Plumb asked to see Roger alone before he introduced him to the clients.

'How are you, Mr Plumb? Do sit down.'

'Very good of you to see us so soon,' said Mr Plumb mournfully as he sat down. 'I must say I'm more than ever glad I came to you in the first instance.' And he wiped his forehead. He waited a moment or two before speaking, and then: 'Mr Thursby, you were quite right, quite right,' he said.

'About what?'

'About the money. I put it to my clients just as you put it to me – about the actual notes being produced by the Chief Constable or the Superintendent or someone – and after a bit they asked if they could have a word together outside my room. When they came back they admitted that what they'd told me hadn't been true. It's most unsettling, Mr Thursby, most disturbing. But what's my duty? I don't pretend I don't want to keep them as clients – as I told you, the conveyancing –'

'Quite,' said Roger.

'But if you tell me to throw them out, I will,' said Mr Plumb. 'Slograve, Plumb have their reputation to think of. That comes first. We've never broken the rules yet.'

'Well, Mr Plumb, in a civil case I think that a solicitor or a barrister is fully justified in throwing out a client who deliberately lies to him. Often in a criminal case, but that isn't always quite so easy.'

'Mr Thursby, there seems to be a slight misunderstanding,' said Mr Plumb, mopping his completely dry brow. 'I don't want to throw them out. I want to know if I've got to.'

'I was coming to that,' said Roger. 'The mere fact that a client tells you a lie certainly doesn't make it necessary for you to refuse to act for him, particularly if he corrects it himself. But, subject to certain general rules, each case has to be judged by itself.'

'General rules, you say? Such as?'

'Well, I expect you know them as well as I do. Have you never been asked – how can you appear for someone whom you know to be guilty?'

'Yes,' said Mr Plumb, 'I have been asked that – more than once.'

'And how d'you answer it?'

'Well, Mr Thursby, to be quite candid, I change the subject. I find it much too difficult. You see, Mr Thursby, my firm doesn't do much criminal work, but, in every case we've handled, I've known the defendant to be guilty, and I feel a little awkward about it, particularly as we got two of them off.'

'D'you mean that your clients admitted to you that they were guilty?'

'Oh, dear me no, Mr Thursby, dear me no. Then it would have been quite simple. We'd just have pleaded guilty. But not a bit of it. They swore blind they were innocent and what's worse, they got away with it. In one case the magistrate swallowed it and in another case the jury.'

'I take it you didn't see them commit the crime yourself, Mr Plumb?'

'I beg your pardon, Mr Thursby? I don't quite follow.'

Roger repeated the question.

'See them do it myself? Of course not. What a question, if I may say so, Mr Thursby.'

'Well,' said Roger, 'if you didn't see them commit the crime and they denied to you that they'd committed it, how did you *know* they'd committed it?'

'Well – it was quite obvious in each case. The evidence was overwhelming.'

'Apparently the jury and the magistrate didn't think so. They're the people to judge, aren't they, not you? You say you *knew* your clients were guilty, but you didn't, you know, you only *thought* it. The judges of the matter thought otherwise. So, as Dr Johnson once said, you were wrong and they were right.'

'I think I see what you're getting at, Mr Thursby.'

'You mustn't put forward what you *know* to be a false case but, subject to that, you must put forward whatever your client's case is, whether you believe in it or not.'

'You make me feel a good deal better, Mr Thursby,' said Mr Plumb, mopping his brow as though he felt a good deal worse.

'When you come to think of it, Mr Plumb,' went on Roger, 'hardly anyone would be defended if his lawyer had to believe in his innocence. If it's any comfort to you, in the few criminal cases I've had I haven't believed in my client's innocence yet.'

'You don't say.'

'I do – at least that's not quite accurate. When I was a very young man I was much more inclined to believe what I was told, and I did once appear for a motorist in whose innocence I passionately believed. She was very pretty, so I may have been prejudiced. It wasn't a very serious matter. She was fined forty shillings. I felt like paying it myself.'

'Well, Mr Thursby, I'd better say at once that I do not – and shall not – feel like going to gaol for Mr and Mrs Glacier – not for all the conveyancing in the world.'

'Hadn't we better have them in?' said Roger, 'or was there something else you wanted to tell me first?'

'Well, there was, but on the whole I think you'd better get it from them yourself. I wasn't very successful in the first instance.'

Roger rang the bell and Donald showed Mr and Mrs Glacier into his room. Mr Plumb introduced them. Mr Glacier was a small bearded man with a slight foreign accent. He had an extremely good command of English but, every now and then, he would use a perfectly correct expression in a manner which suggested that he was uncertain whether it was right. It might well have been an affectation. Mrs Glacier had obviously been very attractive when young. Her knowledge of English was not as good as her husband's – except as regards bridge terminology; she knew all the words necessary to be able to play the game regularly from 3 to 6 p.m.

'Mr and Mrs Glacier,' said Roger, 'I'm sure you'll understand that I'm only here to help you, but I cannot emphasize too strongly the necessity for your telling me the truth and the whole truth. If you don't, I may make things infinitely worse for you.'

'The truth,' said Mr Glacier. 'Ah – who knows it?'

'You and your wife do in this case.'

'Is the world round or flat?' asked Mr Glacier. 'Is the moon made of green cheese?' Mr Glacier paused to see if he had made an impression. Apparently he had. There was silence.

'At one time it was popularly supposed that the world was flat. If a boy at school had said it was round he would not have been telling the truth, as it was then known. Who knows – tomorrow the world may be flat.'

'It may indeed,' said Mr Plumb sadly.

'And green cheese,' continued Mr Glacier, 'is it impossible that it was once believed that the moon *was* made of green cheese? The truth – pah!' said Mr Glacier. 'When you English lawyers talk of the truth you make me –' and he looked round the room as though for a spittoon.

'Mr Glacier,' said Roger, 'I have not the time at the moment for a discussion as to the meaning of truth, but let us assume the earth once was flat and now is round, and that the moon was once made of green cheese and now is made of – I don't think you mentioned what the moon is now made of?'

'Brass,' said Mr Glacier.

'Brass?' queried Mr Plumb.

'No one has been there yet and brought away a – what is the word? – a sample. It could be. Or perhaps I should say you cannot prove it is not.'

'Scientists could,' said Roger.

'Scientists,' said Mr Glacier with an air of triumph, 'the best scientists of the day once were convinced that the earth was flat.'

'Very well, brass it shall be,' said Roger. 'And now shall we get down to the matter in question? All this arose because I wanted you to understand that you may do yourselves a great deal of harm by not telling me the un-varnished —'

'Brass,' put in Mrs Glacier.

'The inside of Holloway Prison is, I believe,' said Roger, 'no more comfortable than that of Wormwood Scrubs. Bribery of the police is a very serious charge. Anyone con-victed of it is very likely to go to prison. Mr Glacier would start at Wormwood Scrubs and Mrs Glacier at Holloway. I'm sorry to put it so crudely, but, unless you treat this matter seriously, you may be sorry later.'

'Very well, sir,' said Mr Glacier, 'put your questions. I will endeavour to answer them with a — how do you say? — a candour that will surprise us both.'

'You are both charged,' said Roger, looking at the sum-monses which Mr Plumb had given him, 'with two offences. It is said that on the 14th December Mr Glacier gave twenty pounds to Inspector Worcester as an inducement to persuade him to withdraw the licensing prosecution or to give false evidence. I understand that you did in fact give the inspector twenty pounds on that occasion.'

'No,' said Mr Glacier.

'But Mr Plumb tells me —' began Roger.

'No,' repeated Mr Glacier.

Roger looked at Mrs Glacier.

'I pass too,' she said.

'Mr Plumb,' said Roger, 'I thought you told me —'

'Ask them again,' said Mr Plumb.

'Did you not give the inspector twenty pounds?' repeated Roger.

'I did not,' said Mr Glacier.

'Either on the 14th December or on any other day?'

'On no occasion did I hand the inspector twenty pounds. My wife will confirm this.'

Roger looked at Mr Plumb, who sat quite calmly, only very occasionally mopping his brow.

'Ask him again,' said Mr Plumb.

'Really,' said Roger, 'I confess I'm getting a little tired of this. Mr Plumb originally informed me that you denied giving any money to the police, but after I had pointed out to him that the actual notes would be produced in Court he told me that you had admitted you had given the money.'

'Can I rely on the money we gave being produced in Court?' asked Mr Glacier.

'I thought you said you hadn't given any.'

'Can I rely on the money we gave being produced in Court?' repeated Mr Glacier.

'You certainly can,' said Roger rather crossly.

'I venture most respectfully to disagree,' said Mr Glacier. 'The money we gave will not be produced in Court – most assuredly it will not be. You may corroborate me, my peach.'

'I collaborate,' said Mrs Glacier.

'Ask me again the question,' said Mr Glacier.

'Did you give the inspector twenty pounds?'

'No,' said Mr Glacier. 'Definitely not.'

A sudden light dawned on Roger.

'How much did you give?'

'Thirty pounds,' beamed Mr Glacier.

'That was the first call,' put in Mrs Glacier.

'Correct, my angel,' said Mr Glacier.

'The second time you're supposed to have given twenty-five pounds,' said Roger. 'How much was it then?'

'Thirty-five pounds,' said Mr Glacier, with obvious enjoyment.

'I suppose there's no corroboration of your story?' said Roger.

'I collaborate,' said Mrs Glacier.

'Yes,' said Roger, 'but I'm afraid you're an interested party. You're charged with the offence.'

'But it's the truth,' said Mr Glacier, adding, after a slight pause, 'this time.'

'Quite,' said Roger, 'but how is one to know? And if I believe you – and it doesn't matter whether I do or I don't – will the jury believe you unless there's something to show that you're telling the truth and the police officers aren't?'

'The jury,' said Mr Glacier, 'will not know of – how shall I say? – the way we first put it to Mr Plumb.'

'That's certainly an advantage,' said Roger.

'I'm afraid,' said Mr Plumb, 'that I'm a little out of my depth. Mr and Mrs Glacier are charged with giving money to the police. They admit it. What defence is it that they gave more than is charged against them?'

'I'll come to that in a moment,' said Roger. 'First of all, I wanted to see whether we'd be likely to establish that you had paid more than is alleged in the summonses.'

'Suppose you can? What then?' said Mr Plumb.

'I rather fancy,' said Roger, 'that the police would be much more interested in prosecuting their own black sheep than in securing a conviction against Mr and Mrs Glacier.'

'You're not suggesting we should tell the police what our clients have admitted to us?' said Mr Plumb, wiping his forehead vigorously.

'I certainly am,' said Roger, 'if it has any chance of being believed and quite likely if it hasn't.'

'Do I understand,' said Mr Glacier, 'that you intend to betray our – what is the word? – our confidences to the police?'

'Of course not,' said Roger. 'Until I know a lot more I don't know what I'm going to advise you. But if I advise you to instruct us to tell the police and you don't want us to do so, of course we shan't tell them. What you tell us is in confidence and if you don't want to take my advice you needn't. Is that plain, Mr Glacier?'

'Then would you explain why you should want at all to tell our case to the police? You will forgive me, Mr Thursby. I am not any longer talking of the earth being round or flat or the moon being made of green cheese or brass or cobalt or anything at all. What I am saying is nothing to do with the moon. Is that plain, sir?'

'Entirely.'

'Well, sir, I do not read many detective stories, nor do I read of very many cases in Court, but in my fifty-seven years I have read something of crime and I do not remember any case where a man's own lawyer has gone to the police – how do you say? – like a lamb to the slaughter – or perhaps I should say has led his client like a lamb to the slaughter.'

'Don't let's worry about detective stories or other cases, Mr Glacier, though, as a matter of fact, there are quite a number of cases where a solicitor has gone to the police with his client to make a confession.'

'I do not propose to make a confession. Why should I present it to them as you say on a plate – like a piece of cake?'

'As I've said before,' said Roger, 'until I know the full facts I can't say what I'm going to advise you, but, as you're so worried about this particular point, let me deal with it. Supposing I do advise you to go to the police and say what has happened, how will it hurt you?'

'*Mon Dieu!* The earth *is* flat,' said Mr Glacier. 'He asks how it will hurt me. You hear that, my cabbage. The moon *is* made of green cheese.'

'I collaborate,' said Mrs Glacier.

'Now listen,' said Roger patiently. 'Let's assume that you don't tell the police anything, what will happen? Both police officers will give evidence that you gave them twenty pounds on the first occasion and twenty-five pounds on the second occasion. Upon that evidence the magistrates are bound to commit you for trial at the Assizes. When it comes to your trial the same thing will happen. The officers will give their story in evidence. If you don't give evidence in your own defence you will obviously be convicted. There'll be nothing to contradict the police evidence, and so the jury will believe them. Do you follow so far?'

Mr Glacier nodded in assent. Mr Plumb paused with his handkerchief in mid-air. He was puzzled and fascinated.

'If, on the other hand, you do give evidence,' went on Roger, 'you will then have to say what you've told me now. If it's got to come out then, how does it hurt you for it to come out earlier?'

This time Mr Plumb nodded in assent. But the effect on Mr Glacier was electric. He looked agonizingly upwards, he tugged at his beard several times, stood up, sat down, stood up again and threw out his arms, sat down and buried his head in his hands. Then he looked imploringly as for comfort to his wife.

'I collaborate,' she said.

'What's the trouble?' asked Roger.

'The world is not flat – it is not round – it is triangular – it is going round very fast indeed – now it is going to stop and we shall all be thrown off.' He cupped his hand to his ear. 'D'you hear those rumblings?' he asked. 'We shall be blown off any minute now.'

Mr Plumb, who had followed Roger's explanations of the situation with complete understanding and some pleasure, now began to mop his forehead vigorously again.

'Mr Glacier,' said Roger, 'I can only imagine that you're troubled at having to tell the truth to the jury.'

'Troubled?' said Mr Glacier. 'That is a good word. Troubled! It is we who rot in gaol, sir, not you or the amiable Mr Plumb – it is we, your clients. If we want to tell the truth to the jury, do we need a lawyer – two lawyers? Please do not think I mind the money. I like money, yes. But I pay your fees willingly if there is some point. But if all you say is go and lift up your chin so that it can be conveniently punched, or place your body in a position where it can be conveniently kicked – well, sir – I can do that without your assistance. I need no help to fall into the river. It is kind of you to offer to give me – how do you say? – a send off, but I can jump – and quite as far and as deep as you can push me – if I want to, sir – but – I do not want to, sir – *I do not want to*, sir. Do I make that plain?'

'I suppose,' said Roger quite calmly, 'that your idea is that we should invent a good story for you to tell.'

'What else is a lawyer for? When the truth is good, what need have I of a lawyer? I go to a lawyer when the truth is – how do you say? – inconvenient.'

'Well,' said Roger, 'there may be some countries where lawyers behave like that. And there may be one or two over here who'd do it for you, but not many, and they'd be kicked out pretty quick if they were found out.'

'There are not many such?' asked Mr Glacier.

'Very few,' said Roger.

'You have their addresses perhaps?' said Mr Glacier.

'I have not,' said Roger. 'I think perhaps Mr Plumb, the time has come –'

Mr Plumb said gloomily : 'I'm afraid Mr Glacier doesn't understand our ways. You see, Mr Glacier, although lawyers in this country have to help their clients, they have to do it honestly.'

'But, of course,' said Mr Glacier. 'That is all I was asking.'

Mr Plumb and Roger tried hard to explain to Mr Glacier what are the duties and responsibilities of lawyers in this country. Roger even repeated part of his earlier advice to Mr Plumb. Mr Glacier tried hard to follow.

'But, let me ask you something,' he said after a little time. 'You wish your client to win the day, do you not?'

'But by proper methods,' interposed Mr Plumb.

'Quite so. But you want to do the best for him?'

'Certainly.'

'Well, gentlemen, let us suppose you have a client charged with murder and you think he has committed the crime. No – I have quite understood this afternoon's lesson – you only *think* he has committed it, you do not *know* it. Now, thinking he has committed it – do you say to him, as you said to me, now tell us the truth? If you are right in thinking him culpable – I mean guilty, of course – he will, will he not, have to admit the crime when he tells you the truth? And, if he tells you that he is guilty, I understand now from you that he will have to say the same to the judge and jury. Is that best for him, gentlemen? Is it even good for him? How hard do you try to persuade your client to tell the truth when you believe the truth will – what is the word? – will condemn him?'

'Mr Glacier,' said Roger, 'this is a very interesting discussion on the ethics of the legal profession, but I'm afraid I haven't time for very much more. If you want me to continue to advise you in your particular case, I will do so – provided you now understand and will stick to the rules. I must make it plain, though, that if you don't, I reserve the right to throw up the case in the middle.'

'I have read of that, now I come to think of it,' said Mr Glacier. 'I am interested to know what it means. I am sorry to have shocked you so much, gentlemen. I confess that you have shocked me. But I think I am, as you say, over it now and I would like you to proceed, if you please.'

'Well, then,' said Roger, 'I'd like you to tell me in your own words how you came to pay this money, what was said when you paid it, where you got the actual money from, and whether there's any means of proving that you paid sixty-five pounds and not forty-five pounds.'

Mr Glacier hesitated for a moment. 'As to proof – beyond my wife's and my own word – I shall have to think, but the rest I can answer now. We run a small club at the Glorious; our daughter is the secretary. The unfortunate matter of drinks after hours strictly concerns the club rather than the hotel. Our daughter, who is young and – you will forgive a father's pride – beautiful, has just become *fiancée* – engaged – unofficially. To someone of importance. It is perhaps not necessary at the moment to mention his name. If she had been prosecuted, it would have been most unfortunate – it might even have prevented the marriage – one cannot say where these things end. We were therefore extremely worried about the matter and, at the time the officers disclosed themselves at the party, the situation was in fact mentioned to them. No hint, I assure you, gentlemen, of money. We just happened to mention how unfortunate it would be if Melanie were charged. You can imagine then how pleased we were to find when the inspector and sergeant came to serve us with the licensing summonses that there was no summons for Melanie. We were overjoyed and we said so. The officers said they were only doing their duty and that Melanie did not – how did they say? – did not come into it. Now, the office in which we interviewed the police contains my safe where, during the day, a fair amount of cash is kept. I felt so pleased – so grateful that, without really thinking anything about it, I opened it, took out a bundle of notes and asked the inspector to accept it with our most distinguished compliments.'

'You say a bundle of notes. How d'you know there were thirty?'

'When I – how do you say? – balanced the cash.'

'You could have made a mistake.'

'Certainly not. Impossible. There is a check for everything. It balanced except for thirty pounds.'

'What did the inspector say?'

'He said it was very kind of us, but we were to remember he had only been doing his duty.'

'How did you come to give the next lot?'

'The inspector came again with the sergeant to prepare a plan of the premises for the Court proceedings. They chatted to us. It was all very friendly. They or I mentioned our daughter. Again we said how grateful we were. Again they said they were only doing their duty. Again I went to the safe. This time I knew it was thirty-five pounds I took out. There was a packet of twenty-five pounds and I took another packet of ten pounds.'

'Why?'

'Why does one do anything? I felt grateful. We are not poor. And then, too, I thought perhaps it was expected of me. The officers stayed rather longer than was necessary.'

'How did you account for the money in your books?'

'Entertainment expenses.'

'Well, I should like to see your books for the day and I'd like your accountant to go through the slips or checks for that day and let me have a report. What I want to find out is if there's any possible corroboration in your books and papers that the extra ten pounds passed each time.'

'To be quite frank with you, sir, I do not think there can be.'

'All the same I'd like it done, please,' said Roger. 'I'm bound to say I find difficulty in accepting what Mr Glacier says in its entirety – he will forgive me in the circumstances for saying so, I hope. If the officers were dishonest, I can't see why they should have put in a charge at all if they'd been given the money like that. They could just have kept it and no one would have been any the wiser. But suppose that what Mr Glacier says isn't entirely accurate. Suppose he did try to bribe the officers – it *is* possible that a dishonest policeman would try to get the best out of both worlds – by reporting the matter to his superior and keeping ten pounds on the way. He would argue to himself that Mr Glacier would probably deny everything – as indeed he did at first and would have done up to the trial, if Mr Plumb and I hadn't intervened. He would feel quite satisfied that at any rate Mr Glacier would never dare to say he had given more than the forty-five pounds mentioned in the summonses. Of course, after he had been convicted he might tell every-thing, but it would be too late then. No one would believe him. So, from a dishonest officer's point of view, it was pretty well a certainty. If we'd got some corroboration and went to the police, I believe there'd be a very good chance of their chasing their own people instead of you. And if they didn't, as I've pointed out, you'd have lost nothing. For better or worse, your story's coming out in the end. Bring it out now and it may do you more good. I think it's worth trying anyway, but we do want something more than your word if we can get it. Mark you, in any event the fact that we tell the police the story at all is fairly strong and will make them think a bit.'

'So you advise?' said Mr Plumb.

'First of all, get someone on to the books at once. There must be no delay at all. Then, in a couple of days I'd advise Mr and Mrs Glacier to authorize you, Mr Plumb, to go straight to the Chief Constable of the County and tell him everything – not in confidence, mind you. Openly. Tell him he can use it as much as he likes.'

'Is that necessary, Mr Thursby?' queried Mr Plumb.

'In my view, yes. In fact, in criminal matters there can be no such thing as without prejudice or the like and, although I've no doubt the Chief Constable would respect your confidence as far as he properly could – which incidentally might not be possible – you can't go to a Chief Constable and say – between you and me, old boy, and you won't let it go any further, but I've murdered my grandmother – although he'd keep it in confidence if he could – you've nothing to gain from his so doing and you may have something to gain from keeping it quite open. For example, we can tell the jury all about it if they go on with the prosecution. But the object, of course, is with luck to stop the prosecution. If we fail in that, as far as I can see, we'll only have done ourselves a bit of good. But it's up to Mr and Mrs Glacier. If they don't like the idea that's an end of it.'

'Mr Thursby,' said Mr Glacier, 'I am beginning to entertain a great respect for you if I may say so. I like the idea.'

'I collaborate,' said Mrs Glacier.

Chapter 6

THE ANCIENT MARINER

━━━

On his way home that evening, rather earlier than usual, Roger was stopped by one of the ancient mariners of the Temple. Their ages vary from something over forty to something under ninety. It is very difficult to get away from any of them, but no one likes to hurt their feelings. So they ply a flourishing trade. If Roger saw any of them far enough off and he considered himself unobserved, he would slip through an arch into another of the Temple's courts; but there are not many long approaches in the Temple and usually he, like everyone else except the really rude men of the Temple, had to submit to the inevitable. There is seldom anything sad about these ancient warriors. Few of them have ever had any practice and must have had independent means to enable them to continue at the Bar. None of them would recognize himself as one of their number and they are completely oblivious of the fact that their victims are wriggling and squirming to get away. Of course, sometimes they meet each other. That is excellent. All they want to do is talk, and they both talk and neither listens and a good time is had by all.

'Haven't seen you for a long time, old boy,' said Roger's captor. 'Done any sketching lately?'

'Not really had much time, as a matter of fact.'

'Ah, you're one of the busy ones – though between you and me I haven't met anyone who isn't. Everyone rushing off to or from a conference or consultation. Strictly between ourselves, old boy, I often suspect the conference is at the Cock and the consultation in the imagination. Not in your case, of course.'

'I'm going home, as a matter of fact.'

'And the best place, too. My home's here. Come up and have a glass of sherry and a yarn.'

'Well, as a matter of fact –'

'Come along, old boy – take your mind off all those briefs. Come on – it's only just up here.' He led the polite and unresisting Roger to his residential chambers.

'I like living over the shop, I must say. Saves an awful lot of time. I bet it takes you at least three quarters of an hour to get home.' Roger conceded that it did.

'There you are, you see. Takes me exactly three minutes. Have a chair. I'll get a couple of glasses.'

Roger waited patiently and wondered how long he would have to endure the punishment. He would refuse a second glass. That was definite.

'Here we are, old boy. Hope you'll like it. Rather a good line I've got from El Vino. I know the manager there rather well and he always lets me have anything rather special. Well – here's luck.'

They sipped the sherry.

'Not bad, eh?'

'Very good. Very good indeed.'

'I had Mervyn here the other day. Said it was the best he'd ever had. He ought to know. He was weaned on sherry. Well, what's the news? Who's going for silk? No one's written to me yet. As a matter of fact, they don't always, you know. I've seen a name or two in the paper – junior to me by years – but not so much as by your leave or with your leave. Oh, well – it's a sign of the times. Mind you, I don't believe anyone's applied just because they've had a note from someone else saying he is. Still I like these old courtesies. But courtesy's out of date, I suppose. Like me.'

'Nonsense,' said Roger. 'Didn't you have that robbery appeal in the Court of Criminal Appeal the other day?'

'Yes.'

'Jolly good,' said Roger, glad that he was right. 'You were successful, I gather?'

The ancient mariner's face fell slightly. 'As a matter of fact I was for the Crown, old boy, and they allowed the appeal. Between you and me I still don't know what they were talking about. Said I oughtn't to have asked one prisoner where he met the other.'

'Where was it?'

'In gaol, of course. How was I to know? Anyway, he only answered "In Devonshire, sir", and I don't suppose the jury knew it was Dartmoor.'

'Bad luck,' said Roger, 'but, as old Grimes would say – they will do these things, they will do these things.'

'Amazing man, old Grimes. Goes on for ever. Just as good as ever. Now *he* never has time for a sherry. But, of course, he hasn't. I don't know how he gets through it all. What you doing tonight? Theatre or something?'

'As a matter of fact, I've got a spot of work.'

The ancient mariner winked. 'I know, old boy,' he said. 'I could do with some myself.'

Chapter 7

CRABTREE

ROGER was in Court all the next morning trying to convince the Court of Appeal that one of its previous decisions had been made *per incuriam* or, as the layman might put it, by a slip of the tongue. He had little success. It is not particularly easy to convince a single judge that his tongue has slipped. It is naturally even more difficult to convince three judges that all their three tongues have slipped and all at approximately the same moment. During a lull in the proceedings, while his opponent was being asked a question, Roger – in a flash of genius – decided that, if one of the Lords Justices should be made a peer, his motto should be '*Per incuriam nihil*,' which, Roger thought, might be translated for the benefit of members of his family who knew no Latin as 'Always conscious of our bloomers'. He was interrupted in these thoughts by the Lord Justice in question :

'Well, Mr Thursby,' he said, 'I can't speak for my brethren, but personally I have no doubt about the matter.'

'My Lord,' said Roger, with a glance at the clock, 'I hope that after lunch I shall have the opportunity first, of infusing some doubt in your Lordship's mind and then, of satisfying your Lordship that my argument is sound.'

'You will require an extremely effective lunch,' said the Lord Justice.

'I'm afraid,' said Roger, 'I shall be lunching on a summons for interrogatories.'

'I hope,' said another Lord Justice, 'you won't seek to administer any interrogatories to us on our previous decision.'

'Oh, my Lord,' said Roger, 'no one is bound to answer any interrogatory which might incriminate him.'

And on that note the Court adjourned for lunch and

Roger, with Donald, went hurriedly to the Bear Garden to do his summons.

'Who's against us?' he asked Donald on the way.

'Now keep calm, sir,' said Donald. 'It's Crabtree.'

'Oh – no,' said Roger. 'No – please not . . . anything but that.'

'Can't you agree it with him?' asked Donald.

'I'll certainly try,' said Roger, 'but I can never understand what he says.'

Miles Crabtree was an extremely nice fellow and everyone liked him, but he suffered from a most serious defect which made it difficult to understand why he ever received a brief. He was practically incapable of saying one complete sentence by itself. His cross-examination of a witness would usually run something like this :

'Now, Mr Sanders,' – and here he would point his finger at the witness and frown slightly in a rather learned manner – which at first terrified an untruthful witness and which was calculated to make any witness feel that some really difficult question was going to be asked; well, it was going to be difficult, but not in the way the witness thought. . . . 'Now, Mr Sanders, I want to ask you about – but so that your Lordship can follow the question would you be kind enough to turn to page 3 of the correspondence. Your Lordship will see there – in any event it's in the pleadings – would your Lordship look at page 2 of the defence – now, Mr Sanders, with regard to the meeting on the 20th January, but before I come to that would you be so good as to explain why – I don't want to trap you in any way – perhaps my learned friend would let the witness have a copy of the correspondence – would you be good enough to explain why – no, it's no good looking for assistance at the back of the Court, and I want a straight answer Yes or No to this question – your Lordship has found the passage? I don't want to be told afterwards you didn't understand the question, Mr Sanders, so I'll make it quite plain and if you've any doubt will you please say so now – will you kindly wait, sir, until I've formulated the question – you needn't think I'm going to be browbeaten as you browbeat my client – will you kindly give me your attention, sir. Have you – and tell me directly one way or the other – did you or did you not at that meeting in January – no, not the one in January – I'm so sorry, my Lord. I got confused with the correspondence – if your Lordship will turn to page 36 – the last sentence but one – no, your Lordship is perfectly right – there is no page 36 – there must be some mistake – oh, no – I have it, my Lord, it's page 26. And now, sir, I think you've had long enough, quite long enough, to answer the question. Will you kindly do so?'

'I'm afraid I haven't followed the question,' says the witness.

'So you haven't followed the question, haven't you?' begins Crabtree.

'I'm afraid I haven't either,' says the judge.

'Oh – I'm so sorry, my Lord. Your Lordship is very patient. If I may refer your Lordship to page 36 – no, page 26 of the correspondence – your Lordship will see there –'

'Mr Crabtree,' says the judge, 'I think it would be better if you asked the witness a question – just one to begin with. I'll do my best to follow.'

'Your Lordship is very good. Very well then, Mr Sanders – you remember that meeting, the one I was referring to, not the one in January – that was a mistake on my part – the one in February, the meeting which is referred to in the correspondence. You know the one I'm talking about, there's no mistake about it, is there? Now, at that meeting there were three of you present. You, Mrs Bole, Mr and Mrs Meadowes – no, that makes four, I'm sorry. There were four people present and what I want to ask you, Mr Sanders, is did any of you at that meeting – any one or more of you, I mean you or Mrs Bole or Mr and Mrs Meadowes – I think there was no one else present – that's been admitted – your Lordship will see that in the particulars delivered on the 14th January last – no, I'm sorry, my Lord, it's in the defence itself under paragraph 7 – oh, no, my Lord, I'm so very sorry – it *is* in the particulars of the 14th January

after all – I had them in the wrong order in my bundle –
I'm so sorry, my Lord. Now, Mr Sanders, this is very important, I shall make a note of your answer – did you, or
Mrs Bole or Mr and Mrs Meadowes – any one of you, I
mean – say anything like this – I don't mean the actual
words – no one expects you to remember the exact words of
a conversation all that time ago, but anything of the kind, I
mean. I'm waiting for your answer, Mr Sanders.'

'Did who say what?' intervenes the judge.

'Oh, my Lord,' says Crabtree, 'I'm so sorry. I thought
I'd asked the witness. Well, Mr Sanders, so that there may
be no doubt at all about it I'll ask you again.'

And so on and on goes Crabtree, the most patient of
judges eventually wishing that either he or Crabtree had
never been born.

It was not, therefore, very surprising that Roger should
be dismayed at the thought of having Crabtree as an opponent. He had altogether fifty minutes in which to deal with
the summons before Master Tiptree, and another one before
Master Peabody and, if possible, to get something to eat. But,
he reflected with some comfort, thank Heaven there'll be an
end of all this if I get silk. He prayed that the Lord Chancellor would give it to him.

'Hullo, my dear fellow,' said Crabtree, as Roger came
into the Bear Garden – so called because a lot of shouting
goes on – though nothing like as much as there used to be.

The noise is comprised of :

First Attendant (in loud voice): First call – Counsel – G. to N.
George and The Glassbottling Co. Ltd.
Graham and Hurst.
The Gargantuan Co. (1953) Ltd, and Blowback, etc. etc.

First Solicitor's Managing Clerk (in loud voice):
Cosset and Green – Cosset and Green.
Anyone here from Cosset and Green?

Second Attendant (in loud voice): First call – Counsel – O to Z.
Orange and Mowbray.
Ostler Ltd and Jones.
Onapoulos and Deep Sea Fishing Co. Ltd, etc. etc.

Second Solicitor's Managing Clerk (in loud voice):
    Briggs and Moulton – Briggs and Moulton.
    Anyone here from Briggs and Moulton?

Add one more attendant for the cases lettered from A to F
and any number of solicitors' managing clerks, and start
them all up together, and you have the Bear Garden.

'I think we're against one another,' said Crabtree.

'Hullo,' said Roger. 'Yes, I'm in a bit of a mess, as a
matter of fact. It may have to be adjourned, if we can't
agree it. Will you agree to any of the interrogatories?'

'Look,' said Crabtree, 'I'd like to help you, but – well – if
you take the first lot – I mean the first six, well five anyway
– I don't personally see how . . . but no doubt I'm wrong, of
course, but, if you ask me it seems to me – you see, on the
pleadings it's quite clear – I mean if –'

'That's all right,' said Roger, 'we'd better let the Master
decide.'

Chapter 8

CORROBORATION

A few days later Roger had an urgent call from Mr Plumb. 'I've had the most extraordinary piece of information,' he said. He wiped his forehead. 'I hardly know what to make of it. Look at this, Mr Thursby. I took this proof myself.'

He handed Roger a typewritten document. It was signed at the bottom : 'Albert Thrussle.' It began : 'Albert Thrussle, police constable in the Carpshire Police, will state :'

'Before you read it I'd better tell you how he came to see me. Yesterday Mr Glacier telephoned me and said that a policeman had called on him and he asked me if he might bring him along to my office. I said yes, of course, and they came. Mr Glacier then told the policeman to tell me what he'd told him and, after he'd told me, I made it into the form of a statement. I read it out to him. He said it was absolutely right and he signed it. He says he's quite prepared to swear to it.'

'I'd better read it,' said Roger.

He read :

I am a police constable in the Carpshire Police. I have been in the Force three years. I know Sergeant Warwick; I meet him sometimes in the police canteen. The other day he was drinking rather a lot of beer and we got chatting. Somehow or other we talked about cases of bribery and, after a bit, he said: 'I'll tell you a thing. If anyone tries to drop you anything – d'you know what to do?' 'Well, I think so,' I said. 'I bet you don't,' he said. 'Well,' I said, 'what is it?' He winked at me and said: 'They always deny it, don't they? O.K. Take a per cent for yourself. No one the wiser. Easy as pie. I've got one on now.'

'Well, what d'you think of it?' said Mr Plumb. 'There's your corroboration for you.'

'It certainly is,' said Roger. 'But why did he come to you, or rather, to the Glaciers?'

'I asked him that. He said he'd heard about the prosecution and he was so disgusted that anyone could behave like that he came straight along and told Mr Glacier.'

'Why didn't he tell his superintendent?'

'I asked him that too. He said that he didn't like to. From what the sergeant said, the inspector must have been in it too. He was quite sure the superintendent knew nothing about it, but he was in fact on very good terms with the inspector. He knew the inspector and sergeant would just deny it, he thought the superintendent would believe them, and he was frightened of getting into trouble.'

'Why isn't he frightened of getting into trouble now?'

'He says he simply had to do something and as he was frightened of going to the superintendent he came to the Glaciers.'

'P'raps,' said Roger, 'he thought the Glaciers might do something for him out of gratitude, if it became too unpleasant in the police force. They're a grateful couple. We know that on their own story.' He thought for a few moments.

'Did you happen to find out what beat P.C. Thrussle was on?'

'I didn't, as a matter of fact.'

'I hope that by coincidence it didn't take in the Glorious.'

'You mean?'

'Just that. Mr Glacier's moral sense is not exactly of the highest. I said I wanted what Mrs Glacier calls "collaboration". We've got it now with a vengeance. I hope it came of its own accord, and without any assistance from Mr Glacier. I wouldn't put it past them. One of us will have to ask them point blank. I will, if you like; it sounds a bit offensive.'

'That's extremely good of you, Mr Thursby. I must confess I should feel a little hesitation in asking my own client whether he'd been – whether he'd been . . . well, whatever it is you think he may have been doing.'

'I don't think one way or the other, Mr Plumb,' said Roger. 'But, having regard to our previous experience of the Glaciers and their ideas about the truth and what you go to lawyers for, it wouldn't be right to act on this without taking every reasonable precaution first. I'm not at all sure that I shan't make an exception and see the policeman myself. I'll have to think that one out. I suggest you bring the Glaciers to me once again as soon as possible, and I'll let you know if I want the policeman as well.'

'Glacier's in London today, I know,' said Mr Plumb. 'I'll get his wife as well if possible – that's if you can see us.'

'I'll arrange it somehow.'

Mr Plumb left hurriedly.

'What *is* all this?' said Donald. 'I've got to fit in Fitcham and Grant some time. You seem to like the Glaciers. Sure you wouldn't like me to offer them a bed?'

'They're more likely to offer me one,' said Roger. 'They own a lot of hotels, in particular the Glorious at Westlea.'

'I've stayed there,' said Donald, 'when Consultation was running at Annington. Didn't care much for it. Too many visitors and they don't serve beer in the lounge. I'd have left, only we couldn't get in anywhere else. I'll charge them an extra con. for that.'

Donald was looking at the diary as he was speaking. 'All right, you can see them at six, if you like. How long are you going to be? Finish by tomorrow? D'you want me to wait, or will David do?'

'Oh – don't you wait, Donald. I don't suppose we'll be too long. If we are, I expect David can go too and I'll shut up. Tell him to give me a ring if he wants to get away.'

'Thank you, sir. Oh – that'll be old Park,' said Donald, as the bell rang. 'You'd better get back to your room. I want to have a word with him about a fee.'

Roger went back to his room, and Mr Park was admitted by the junior clerk and brought to Donald.

'How are you, Mr Park?' said Donald. 'He's all ready for you.'

'Remarkable,' said Mr Park, 'quite remarkable. The busier a set of chambers, the less you have to wait.'

'Organization, sir,' said Donald modestly.

'Now, I used to go to – well, I won't say where – but somewhere else – and I never had a conference on time. I didn't so much mind myself as I used to send a clerk in the end, but it's the clients, you know, they don't like it. Some people think it impresses. So busy, we have to keep you waiting. Fiddlesticks! I'll tell you what impresses. Conference fixed for two o'clock, conference held at two o'clock.'

'I quite agree with you sir,' said Donald. 'It's just a little matter of arranging. Would you like to go in now, sir? I think you said the clients weren't coming?'

Donald made as if to take Mr Park to Roger – and then stopped: 'Oh, just one thing, as you're here, sir. I would have mentioned it to your clerk, but as you're here perhaps you won't mind. The fee in the Longworthy case, sir. I know the other side have only got seventy-five, but I really can't let Mr Thursby do it single-handed for less than a hundred and fifty.'

'A hundred and fifty?' queried Mr Park. 'That's a bit steep, isn't it? I could get a leader for a good deal less.'

'Of course you could sir, and between you and me, sir, I wish you would. It's putting a lot on Mr Thursby to do this by himself. He's got a great deal on at the moment.'

'Of course he has,' said Mr Park, 'but I want him to do this himself. Between you and me – apart from just a very few at the top – there isn't a leader to touch him. He'll be taking silk himself soon, I suppose?'

'Silk, sir?' said Donald. 'I don't know anything about that, sir.'

'If you did, you wouldn't tell me. Frightened of my taking my junior work away too soon, eh?'

'Well, I suppose he'll have to take it sometime, but he hasn't said a word about it to me at the moment, sir.'

'I believe you,' said Mr Park, 'though I can't think why.'

'Sir,' said Donald, in a tone of injured innocence. 'Well,

would you like to go in, sir? That's all right about the fee, is it, sir?'

'Make it a hundred.'

'I couldn't really, sir. I'm having to return work as it is. I'll tell you what, sir, for old time's sake I'll make it a hundred and thirty.'

'That's a curious fee,' said Mr Park.

'I thought you might say that, sir,' said Donald. 'All right, sir. A hundred and twenty-five. That's settled then, sir. Will you come along now, sir?'

He showed Mr Park into Roger's room.

As soon as that conference – which was about a yacht – was over, Roger had to turn his attention to the comparatively simple matter of an accident on the Kingston by-pass. By six o'clock he was ready for the Glaciers. Only Mr Glacier came this time, accompanied by Mr Plumb.

'Now, about this policeman, Mr Glacier,' began Roger . . .

'Is it not magnificent?' interrupted Mr Glacier. 'From the gods it came, from the gods themselves.'

Roger checked himself from saying he hoped their name wasn't Glacier.

'You asked for corroboration – and there was none – and now – how do you say? – hey presto, you have the most beautiful exquisite corroboration – and all dressed in blue. Are you not pleased, Mr Thursby?'

'Mr Glacier,' said Roger, 'you must forgive my asking you this question, but I'm afraid it's necessary. This is a serious matter for you, and it's also a serious matter for the sergeant and inspector – very serious indeed. Before I'm a party to putting forward your allegations, I want to be as sure as I can that they're true.'

'Ah, we are back to the truth again – to the moon and the earth. I forget how we left them – brass or green cheese – flat or round.'

'I'm afraid that kind of thing doesn't impress me,' said Roger, 'not favourably, anyhow. What I want to ask you, Mr Glacier, is, first of all, whether Constable Thrussle was a complete stranger to you before he came to see you the other day?'

'A complete stranger? As far as I know, yes. I may have seen him in the street, just as I may have seen you in the street before – but I am not aware of having seen either of you.'

'Then you'd never spoken to him before?'

'Subject to the same – how do you say? – qualification, certainly not. I may have met him in a train and asked for a light, or on a country road and said "good evening" – just as I may have said either to you, Mr Thursby, but I am not aware of it in either case. You see how careful I have become since we first met.'

'So it was a surprise to you when he came to see you?'

'A complete surprise.'

'And presumably to your wife too?'

'Absolutely. We looked upon it as manna from heaven. But I assume from your questions that you are wondering whether one of us put the manna there in the first place.'

'Perfectly correct,' said Roger. 'If it's true that you bribed two policemen you might easily bribe a third.'

'Logical, Mr Thursby, but fortunately not so. Why do you not send for the policeman and ask him questions? My English is not as good as his, my understanding of English ways is also not as good as his. Why not put your questions to him? After all, if he has been bribed by me we are both … both – what you call crooks – and it should not take long for a man of your experience to find it out.'

'I had thought of seeing him, Mr Glacier, but it is not normally proper for counsel to see the witnesses in a case – except his own clients. I'm entitled to make an exception to the rule if I think there's a good reason for doing so. At the moment, in view of the advice I'm going to give you, I don't think there is. I've seen the officer's signed statement, I've heard from Mr Plumb how it was taken, and I think I must be satisfied with that.'

'And you are going to advise?'

'What I originally indicated. I think Mr Plumb should go

and see the Chief Constable and tell him everything quite openly, and show him the policeman's statement. What happens after that will depend entirely on the Chief Constable.'

'You want me to go and see the Chief Constable?' asked Mr Plumb rather anxiously, and mopping his brow several times. 'I confess I should find that rather embarrassing. Would it by any chance be possible for you to accompany me?'

Roger thought for a moment. 'If you really want me to do so, I don't see any objection to it. It will be rather inconvenient, but I'll speak to Donald about it, if you like.'

'I should be most grateful if you would,' said Mr Plumb. 'I think it so important that a proceeding of this kind should start off on the right foot, and I might say something of which you would disapprove.'

'I'm sure you wouldn't,' said Roger, 'but, if it'll make you any easier, I'll try to come and start the ball rolling. Of course it may not roll.'

'I have a feeling,' said Mr Glacier, 'that it will roll.'

Chapter 9

TRAFFIC BLOCK

===

ROGER agreed to go with Mr Plumb to see the Chief Constable on the following Saturday. They were to meet independently outside the Chief Constable's house, as Roger was coming from London and Mr Plumb from the country.

'It's a shame your having to leave so early on a Saturday,' said Mrs Thursby.

'I quite agree, Mother,' said Roger, 'but there it is – they will do these things.'

'I suppose they will,' said Mrs Thursby. 'What things?'

'Make work for lawyers. Just as well, I suppose. If everyone were reasonable and good there'd be no need for us.'

'Is the person you're going down to Westlea to see reasonable and good?'

'I'm going for two people really. Mr Plumb, I should say, was certainly good and moderately reasonable. Mr Glacier is logical, if not reasonable, but I suspect that he is pretty bad.'

'I can't think why you bother to act for him then, Roger. There must be plenty of good ones to defend.'

'I doubt it, Mother. Very few innocent people stand in the dock.'

'How horrible,' said Mrs Thursby. 'I'm glad I don't have anything to do with it. I could never defend anyone if I weren't sure of his innocence.'

'Lucky you didn't go to the Criminal Bar, Mother. You'd have felt the draught a bit. Now, I must be off. Bye-bye ... not sure what time I'll be back. I'll ring you if I'm going to be late for dinner.'

Ten minutes later he was on the way to Carpshire. It was not a very long journey, but it was a bad day for driving. Sporting events, roads up, experimental white lines being painted and the like made the traffic in places a seething mass. It did not worry Roger very much. There was plenty of time and it gave him a rest. He turned the wireless on and prepared to enjoy himself for whatever the length of the journey might be. He had just started to accelerate out of a prolonged traffic block when a small car came in fast from a side turning and would have caused a collision if Roger had not happened to have a reaction time quicker than the average mentioned in the Highway Code. The two cars stopped with half an inch between them.

'Really !' said Roger.

'So sorry,' said the girl driver. 'It was my fault. I'm always doing that.'

'You may not be so lucky another time,' said Roger.

'I really oughtn't to –' began the girl, when the sound of impatient hooters from behind made them both drive on. Ten minutes later they stopped next to each other again, but this time it was simply a traffic block. The girl noticed Roger first.

'– drive,' she said.

'I beg your pardon ?' said Roger.

'I was finishing the sentence,' said the girl.

'How did it begin ?'

'What a short memory you've got. Just as well, as a matter of fact.'

Roger now began to notice that she was attractive, about thirty and with a voice he liked.

'Well, remind me please, if it isn't a nuisance.'

'What I said was –'

Again hoots from behind put an end to the conversation. It was another ten minutes before it could be continued. As soon as they were stationary side by side again the girl went on. 'I really oughtn't to –' But this time they did not wait for the hoots, and it was another several minutes before she was able to add '– drive.'

'Why not ?' said Roger.

'Well, it's like this,' said the girl, and they moved on again. About a mile later Roger said :

'Like what?'

'I'll tell you,' said the girl, and the traffic at once started off, this time rather faster than before and for longer. It was ten or twelve minutes before she was able to go on : 'I haven't the qualities of a good driver.'

Roger had time to say : 'I should think you must have a lot of others to make up for it,' before they went on again. Five minutes later : '– if I may say so,' he added.

'Thank you,' she said, and on they went.

At the next stop : 'Are you going far?' asked Roger.

'I'm going to –' but, though she said the word and Roger hoped it was Westlea, he did not really hear it. But she justified his hopes at a level crossing : '– Westlea.'

'So am I.'

'How curious.'

'Isn't it?'

'You wouldn't have –'

Five minutes later : '– lunch with me, I suppose?'

'It ought to be the other way round, really.'

'I shouldn't mind either way. But why?'

'As compensation for nearly running into you.'

'I'm very grateful to you.'

Prolonged hooting put an end to that part of the conversation. It was continued ten minutes later near a bridge which was being repaired. Roger had never been so pleased before to see the sign 'One-way traffic ahead.' He had never thought that he would have been on the look-out for any indication that was likely to produce a traffic block. It is a novel sensation for a motorist. But the girl in the car was giving him a novel sensation too.

'Have you ever picked anyone up in a traffic block before?' she asked.

'I've never even thought of it before.'

'Are you going to Westlea for the week-end?'

'Well no, as a matter of fact I'm going on business.'

'On a Saturday? How boring. I won't work on Saturday.'

'You're going for the week-end, I suppose?'

'Well – yes. My father lives there and I go down some-times.'

'Where will you lunch with me?'

'If you really mean it – at the Glorious, I suppose. That's the best place.'

'Oh –' said Roger, 'isn't there anywhere else?'

'Why – don't you like it?'

'Well – I haven't been there, as a matter of fact ... it's just – oh, well, I don't suppose it matters. My client owns the place.'

'Your client? You an architect?'

'No.'

'Solicitor?'

'No.'

'I give it up.'

The traffic moved on, and this time the high average speed it maintained was, from Roger's point of view, just too bad. 'Don't see why everyone's in such a confounded hurry,' he said to himself. 'Traffic blocks are good for people. This craze for speed, and getting on! It's absurd, and most incon-venient at the moment.' It was a long time before he had another chance, but it came in the end.

'One o'clock at the Glorious, then?'

'All right, if you really mean it. You will be there, I sup-pose?'

'I shall be there,' said Roger. 'Your father's retired, I suppose?'

'Do I look as old as that?'

'No – I meant ... I mean –' Roger collected himself be-fore he started talking like Crabtree. 'You said he lived down there, and I just assumed he'd retired. It was ridiculous, I agree.'

'He's the Chief Constable, as a matter of fact,' said the girl. 'Don't forget there's a fifteen-mile speed limit along the front – and he's very particular about it.'

Chapter 10

COLONEL MADDERLEY

ROGER duly kept his appointment with Mr Plumb outside the Chief Constable's house.

'I was afraid you might be late,' said Mr Plumb. 'I'm told the traffic is terrible.'

'Oh, it's not too bad,' said Roger. 'Hope I haven't kept you waiting.'

'I always like to be a few minutes early,' said Mr Plumb, 'so I'm used to waiting, but I've had quite a pleasant little stroll – except,' he added, 'that I was nearly knocked down by a car.'

'Not by any chance a small grey saloon with a girl driver?' asked Roger.

'It was certainly a woman,' said Mr Plumb.

'Was she all right?' asked Roger, a little too anxiously.

'All right? All right? How do you mean?'

'I mean there wasn't an accident? The car didn't hit anything – or overturn or anything?'

'No, Mr Thursby – the only thing that was nearly overturned was me.'

'I'm glad it was nothing worse,' said Roger.

'So am I,' said Mr Plumb. 'If I could recognize the woman, I'd report her to the police. It was quite disgraceful. She came from a side turning . . .'

'From a side turning?'

'From a side turning,' repeated Mr Plumb, 'as though she owned not only that turning and the main road but part of the pavement as well.'

'Terrible,' said Roger, 'but you wouldn't be able to recognize her again, I gather? Too bad,' he added, cheerfully.

'I didn't say so,' said Mr Plumb. 'I said *if* I could recognize the woman I'd report her. It's a small world, coincidences do happen. I might run into her somewhere.'

'Then you remember what she looked like?'

'You seem to take a remarkable interest in this young woman, Mr Thursby.'

'Then you saw she was young?' said Roger. 'It's just in the blood, I suppose, Mr Plumb. We always cross-examine everyone when they tell us anything. Very bad form. I'm sorry.'

'Not at all,' said Mr Plumb, 'I don't mind your asking questions in the least. On the contrary, it helps to clear my mind; I'm not very observant, you know, and it's possible this little chat of ours will have helped to make the vision on my mind less blurred. You see – I can't describe the woman at all . . . I've no idea whether she was fair or dark, wearing a hat or not – or, indeed, anything about her, but if I see her again I may recognize her instantly. As a matter of fact, I'd started to think about the Glaciers and, if we hadn't had our little talk about it, the vision might have become too blurred to recognize again. But I have a feeling now that I shall be able to do it. Let's hope we meet her. Stranger things have happened.'

'Indeed they have,' said Roger. 'Don't you think we might go in now?'

The Chief Constable of Carpshire, Colonel Madderley, was ready for them. 'Sit down gentlemen, please. What can I do for you?'

Mr Plumb cleared his throat – the sign of a nervous advocate. Roger had done it for some little time twelve years previously and then suddenly, noticing it in other people, he found he did it himself. He stopped the habit instantly. If necessary he cleared his throat a moment or two before he got up to speak.

'Colonel Madderley,' said Mr Plumb, 'I act, as I told you when I made the appointment, for Mr and Mrs Glacier; and Mr Thursby is our counsel. I've asked him to be present at this interview and, indeed, to do the talking. In the special circumstances I thought it advisable. Perhaps, Mr Thursby, you wouldn't mind going on from there?'

'Certainly,' said Roger. 'Chief Constable, I want to make it plain at the outset that we are not asking you to treat in confidence what we tell you. As far as our clients and we are concerned, you may make whatever use you think proper of the information we give you.'

'Sounds very fair,' said the Chief Constable. 'Will you tell me the catch now or later, or do I have to find it out for myself?'

'There's no catch, Chief Constable, I assure you,' said Roger.

'Bait with no hook, eh?' said Colonel Madderley. 'You're not a fisherman, I gather?'

'Not today anyway, Chief Constable,' said Roger. 'The position is this.'

Roger then proceeded to tell Colonel Madderley the story told him by Mr and Mrs Glacier. As soon as he disclosed that more money had passed hands than was alleged in the charges, the Colonel's attitude changed and he became extremely interested. When this was followed by P.C. Thrussle's statement, he got up from his chair and walked up and down once or twice.

'Mr Thursby,' he said eventually, 'I don't trust your clients an inch. If you ask me – I don't expect you to agree – they're a couple of scoundrels. But scoundrels outside the police force are two a penny. Scoundrels inside the police force – and in particular the Carpshire police force – are very rare indeed. I'd sooner out one crooked policeman than convict fifty Glaciers. We're bound to get a bad hat in now and then, but, on the whole, the force is clean and, as long as I'm Chief Constable of Carpshire, the Carpshire force is going to stay clean.'

Mr Plumb cleared his throat. The Colonel, recognizing the signs, held up his hands for silence.

'Forgive me, sir. I want to make the position plain. I wouldn't hang a dog on the word of your clients – forgive my language, and I don't expect you to agree – but it isn't just what *they* say ... it isn't just what Thrussle says, though that's serious enough ... it's the whole bag of tricks put together – it sounds right. I don't profess to be a clever man, gentlemen. I'm not; that's why they made me Chief Constable. But one gets a feeling in things – a sort of woman's intuition – and that's what I've got now. Don't misunderstand me – I may be quite wrong – and don't think that people in Carpshire get arrested because the Chief Constable thinks he has a woman's intuition. Not at all. When I get a feeling like this I follow it up – that's all; and if it leads nowhere, then I was wrong – that's all – and no harm done. I'm going to follow this up–and if I'm wrong I'll be damned glad, but if I'm right, we'll boot that inspector and sergeant out so far that they certainly won't be able to find their way back. Don't think I'm condemning them unheard; I'm not, but . . . well, I won't say any more at the moment about that. Now, I'll tell you what I'm going to do, gentlemen; you may think I'm acting swiftly – well, I was brought up that way . . . shoot first and explain afterwards. I'm going to get straight on to Scotland Yard and, if they agree, as no doubt they will, with you and your clients' cooperation we'll deal with master inspector and master sergeant. Now, I think you wanted to say something, sir,' and the Colonel turned towards Mr Plumb – who had by now completely forgotten what it was.

'I'm sorry, sir,' said the Colonel, 'but you'll forgive me saying that if it was worth saying it was worth remembering. I'm a blunt man, gentlemen, as you'll find if you see much more of me.'

'My clients will certainly cooperate to the full,' said Roger, 'and so will Mr Plumb, I'm sure.'

'It's odd the Glaciers telling you to make a clean breast of it. That type doesn't usually. They lie like troopers, but I suppose you advised them to do so. Damned good advice, if I may say so. They're damned lucky.' He paused momentarily. In his mind's eye he could almost see the inspector and sergeant being flung out of the police force. 'Damned lucky,' he repeated, 'but I'd sooner your clients had the laugh of us than we kept one man in the force we couldn't trust. I don't care whether he's a flattie or a superintendent.

You've got to be able to trust them. Same in the Army. But I won't bore you with that, gentlemen. Still, I did have a corporal once – now, really, I mustn't. My daughter keeps me in order when I'm off duty, but the superintendent doesn't like to. And I don't blame him. I'd give him hell if he tried.'

'Is there anything further you want of us?' asked Roger.

'Not at the moment, gentlemen, but, unless I'm very much mistaken, there will be. As soon as I've heard from Scotland Yard, I'll get in touch with you and let you know the plan of campaign. I won't anticipate what they'll suggest, but I've a very shrewd idea what it will be. Now, might I have your telephone number, please?'

'Mr Plumb will give you his,' said Roger. 'Mr Plumb wanted me to come down on this first occasion but, although I shall no doubt be advising him, I don't think it desirable that I should have any active part in any possible operations. Questions of giving evidence might even arise.'

'Mr Thursby,' said Colonel Madderley, 'you will not, I hope, think I am being fulsome when I say that I think Mr and Mrs Glacier – and Mr Plumb – are very lucky to have your services. You seem, if I may say so, to think two jumps ahead.'

'That's very kind of you,' said Roger. 'I hope you don't still think there's a concealed hook.'

Colonel Madderley laughed. 'How do I know?' he said. 'The fish doesn't know until it's caught him. But, make no mistake, you'll find I struggle like hell – if there is one. Ever tried to catch a twenty-pounder? You'd know if you had.'

After a few more pleasantries, Roger and Mr Plumb left the Chief Constable.

'Magnificent,' said Mr Plumb, as they reached the street. 'Magnificent. I am most grateful to you, most grateful. I should never have put it like that – never. But, now that the ice is broken, I think I shall be able to manage quite comfortably.'

'I'm sure you will,' said Roger, 'but keep in touch with me

all the time. If necessary, ring me at home. You know my number.'

'That's most kind. Now, will you do me the honour of lunching with me?'

'I should have loved to,' said Roger, 'but, as a matter of fact, I arranged to lunch with a friend.'

'Well – perhaps you'll have a drink with me before lunch? Where are you lunching, may I ask?'

'Well, as a matter of fact,' said Roger, blushing in spite of his efforts not to do so, 'it's at the Glorious.'

'Splendid,' said Mr Plumb. 'I was going to report to the clients there, anyway. I'm sure they'll want your lunch to be on the house. They'd be most ungrateful if they didn't. I suggest you bring your friend to the bar. I take it you've no objection to a glass of sherry before lunch?'

'That's most kind,' said Roger uncomfortably. Able as he was at getting clients out of difficulties, he did not see any way out of his own. He hoped that either Mr Plumb wouldn't recognize his aggressor or that, by a further coincidence, there was another girl in the area who drove like . . . 'Now – I wonder what her name is,' he said to himself.

'It's a girl, as a matter of fact,' said Roger, blushing again.

'Delighted,' said Mr Plumb, 'if you've no objection – and, of course, if she hasn't either.'

'I'm sure she'd be very pleased. Shall we meet in the lounge?'

They drove separately to the Glorious, but arrived almost at the same time. They parked their cars and went up the steps to the hotel together.

'Will she be there?' wondered Roger, not certain in the circumstances whether he hoped she would or wouldn't be. He soon knew. She was. He went straight up to her with Mr Plumb. 'Hullo,' he said, 'may I introduce – Mr Plumb, Miss Madderley.' He swallowed the name Madderley so successfully that Mr Plumb did not hear it. But the girl did. In a surprised voice . . . 'How –' she began, and then quickly altered it into 'do you do?'

'How d'you do?' said Mr Plumb and then, as Roger had feared he might, looked curiously at the girl.

'Surely we've met somewhere before,' he said.

'Then it was you,' she said. 'I'm terribly sorry. I nearly ran into you. I do hope it didn't give you an awful shock. There really ought to be some warning at the junction.'

'There is a kerb,' said Mr Plumb, recollection of his near escape and anger making him bold.

'Yes,' she said, 'there is, of course. I oughtn't to have gone over it. I am so sorry. I wonder why I do these things? Anyway, I'm so glad there are no bones broken.'

'Miss . . . I'm afraid I didn't quite catch your name – I'm only so sorry to have to say this to a friend of Mr Thursby – but –'

'Miss Madderley,' said Roger, 'is daughter of the Chief Constable of Carpshire.'

'Bless my soul,' said Mr Plumb. 'I see. I see. Oh, I see. Well – but . . . but you didn't appear to know her father.'

'I didn't until this morning,' said Roger.

'I see,' said Mr Plumb, 'but you didn't mention you knew his daughter.'

'We had other things to talk about, Mr Plumb, if you remember,' said Roger. 'What about that drink you promised us?'

'Of course, I'm so sorry,' said Mr Plumb, and led them to the bar.

'Have you been to see my father?' said the girl.

'I'm afraid I have,' said Roger and, as Mr Plumb was slightly ahead of them, added under his breath : 'I know it's a bit soon.'

PAPER WORK

══════

THE next day – Sunday – Roger went to church. He had not done so on an ordinary Sunday for a long time.

'How nice,' said his mother, 'but is anything the matter?'

'Nothing unpleasant,' said Roger.

After church he spent an hour working before lunch, drafting Statements of Claim beginning with something like this :

The Plaintiff is and was at all material times the owner of a Jersey cow. The Defendant is and was at all material times the owner of a Standard motor car, index number 999 ZYX.

Somewhere in the middle of the Statement of Claim the two met. Animal lovers will be pleased to know that the penultimate paragraph showed that the cow completely recovered. The cost of convalescence, however, was considerable. This was explained in detail and a claim was made for all the expense to which the plaintiff had been put and for the inconvenience he had suffered, Jersey milk being unobtainable in the neighbourhood and the plaintiff having to be satisfied with something less beneficial to his health, as a result of which he had lost weight. Most people today would have given a small credit for this, but not so the plaintiff. It turned out that it was most important for him to maintain his weight. He did not claim for the loss at so much a pound, but included this claim under the general heading of 'damages'. The total amount was unspecified – such a pity if you claim too little – looks bad if you claim too much. 'Damages' covers everything from a farthing to a million pounds or more. Nothing was claimed for the inconvenience to the cow, unless this could be considered as coming within the last words in Roger's claim which were 'further or other relief'. He had asked for this in innumerable statements of claim, but he had never yet had a case in which they had done anybody any good. But it cost nothing to put them in and perhaps one day he would be glad they were included.

Having dealt satisfactorily and expeditiously with the cow and the motor car, Roger proceeded to draft a defence on behalf of a business man who was alleged to owe money to a company. Many and varied were the defences he raised. The money had never been borrowed or if it had (which was denied) it had been paid back; the company had no power to lend money; the money if paid to the defendant at all (which was denied) was really repayment of capital which was illegal and so much the worse for the company; and finally, having denied everything which was alleged against his client, he added 'Save in so far as has been hereinbefore expressly admitted' – and here it may be remarked that nothing whatever had been admitted – 'the defendant denies each and every allegation in the Statement of Claim contained as fully as if the same had been herein set forth and specifically traversed.'

Having settled these two documents, Roger just had time before lunch to draft a letter for his solicitor to send in a case which involved carrots and linseed oil.

Then he had lunch, an hour's nap and back again to his paper work. And, of course, he must get ready for that non-jury case on Monday. What a pity he hadn't a leader in it. However, there it was – and, with luck, there wouldn't be too many Sundays on which he would have to do this again. He would be a leader himself – with time – with time for Anne.

Chapter 12

CONFERENCES

A FEW days later Mr Plumb called on Roger with news of the Glacier case. He was almost cheerful.

'It's going very well, Mr Thursby, very well indeed. I've been down to see the Chief Constable again.'

'Well, what's happening?'

'It's been arranged that Mr Glacier shall be provided with marked notes with which he is to try to bribe the inspector and sergeant again. So as to avoid arousing their suspicion, the prosecution is to go on just the same but, if the officers fall into the trap, it'll be dropped.'

'Well,' said Roger, 'that's almost as good as we can get. When's the first hearing?'

'Next Friday week. I've arranged with your clerk for you to be there.'

'Who's prosecuting, d'you know?'

'Well – they're not sure. But I think they're going to take in a leader.'

'What's the object of that?'

'The Chief Constable says they did so in the last bribery case and he thought they'd better do the same again so as to avoid any possibility of the officers tumbling to what has happened. And I'll tell you two other things.'

Roger had never seen Mr Plumb so happily excited.

'Yes?'

'They're going to have plain-clothes detectives in and round the Court throughout the proceedings, in case our client gets a chance to give them something.'

'I shouldn't have thought they'd take anything like that. Still, I suppose they know what they're doing. What was the other thing you were going to tell me?'

'Most interesting. D'you know what he said to me?'

'The Chief Constable?'

'Yes. He said he'd suspected the inspector for a long time and would be damned glad to get him. They'd never had any evidence before.'

'That's useful,' said Roger. 'If things go wrong, we may be able to use that.'

'I'm afraid we can't,' said Mr Plumb.

'I think we can,' said Roger. 'I think it'll be admissible in evidence. But let's hope it doesn't arise.'

'But we can't use it, Mr Thursby,' said Mr Plumb. 'It was told me in confidence.'

'What do you mean?' said Roger, rather crossly. 'I told the Chief Constable from the start that there was no question of confidence on our side. Nor can there be on his unless he said so.'

'He did say so,' said Mr Plumb.

'Well – why on earth didn't you tell him there was no question of confidence either way?'

Mr Plumb brought out his handkerchief. 'I'm sorry if I've done the wrong thing, Mr Thursby,' he said, becoming mournful for the first time at that conference.

'It is rather aggravating,' said Roger. 'I thought I'd made it quite plain from the start. It's ridiculous that they should be able to use anything we say and that we can't use what they say. How did it happen?'

'It was like this,' said Mr Plumb, mopping away, 'it was like this. Nothing whatever had been said about confidence, I assure you, Mr Thursby. Then he told me what I've told you about his suspecting the inspector.'

'Well, where does the confidence come in?' asked Roger, brightening slightly.

'After he'd said it,' said Mr Plumb unhappily, 'he added "that's in confidence, of course".'

'And what did you say?'

Mr Plumb wiped his forehead vigorously and, after a few moments of this, looked hard at the ground and, in his most doleful voice, said: 'I'm afraid I said "of course".'

Roger sighed. 'Oh, dear,' he said.

'It took me by surprise,' said Mr Plumb. 'I never thought about it. He said "that's in confidence, of course", and I just said "of course". It's easy to be wise after the event, Mr Thursby, but I really don't know what else I could have done.'

'I agree it was difficult,' said Roger, 'but it is a pity you didn't remind him of what we'd said in the first instance; however, there it is. It's no use crying over spilt milk. And anyway, if all goes well it won't matter.'

'I'm sorry you think I did wrong, Mr Thursby. It shows how right I was to have had you there in the first instance. If you'd been there this time it would never have happened. I'm so sorry, Mr Thursby.'

'Never mind,' said Roger, 'most people would have done the same.'

'Then you don't think it amounted to negligence on my part?' said Mr Plumb. 'We'd better inform our insurance company, hadn't we?'

'Good heavens, no,' said Roger. 'Of course it didn't amount to negligence. At the most it amounted to an error of judgement. Some people might even say you were quite right.'

'I wish you were one of them, Mr Thursby.'

'Don't take it to heart, Mr Plumb. I've done far worse things in my time.'

'Thank you, Mr Thursby, that's very generous.'

'Well, I'll see you on Friday week then,' said Roger, 'at the Magistrate's Court. One thing I must know before then. Is it agreed with the prosecution that I should withhold my cross-examination altogether? Or am I to behave just as I should in the ordinary way? That's very important. I must know that quite definitely. I'll have a word with their counsel, of course, but I'd like to know before I see him what the form is.'

'You shall know,' said Mr Plumb. 'Oh, dear – I do hope I don't make any more mistakes.'

Mr Plumb went back to his office and Roger picked up the papers for his next conference – *Streak v. Broad*. He had just opened them when Donald showed in his solicitor, Mr Glade, and the client — a smart gentleman of about Roger's age.

'I've asked for this conference,' said Roger, 'because quite frankly I don't understand this case at all. Mr Streak apparently has some claim for commission against the defendant, but I can't follow what it is and I couldn't possibly draft a Statement of Claim on these instructions.'

'I shouldn't worry,' said Mr Streak. 'He won't defend; he can't.'

'I dare say,' said Roger, 'but I must know what you're claiming.'

'A lot of money, Mr Thursby,' said Mr Streak, 'and he's got it. I've seen it. And he'll pay. He'll have to.'

'But what is the commission you're claiming?'

'Oh — we had a lot of deals together. Just put in anything — he'll pay.'

'If I'm to draft a Statement of Claim I must know what the deals were, how they were made, what were their terms, and so on. We'd better take them one by one. What was the first?'

'This is really quite unnecessary,' said Mr Streak. 'Let me show you something.' Mr Streak opened an attaché case and brought out a number of documents. He handed one to Roger.

'What's this?' asked Roger.

'It's a photostat,' said Mr Streak.

'So I see,' said Roger, 'but of what?'

'Of the minutes of a board meeting which was never held for a company which didn't exist.'

'I don't follow,' said Roger.

'D'you see who was present?' said Mr Streak. 'Lord Mount, Sir Herbert Pennyfeather and the rest.'

'I wish you'd tell me what this is all about,' said Roger. 'I'm not surprised Mr Glade's instructions are unintelligible if this is how he had to get them.'

Mr Streak winked.

'That meeting was held in the imagination of Mr Broad

only. That's his handwriting. He had five thousand pounds from Mrs Plant on the strength of that piece of paper. I bought it back from her for two thousand five hundred pounds – Mr Broad's money of course – and I gave it him back. But I took the precaution of having this made of it first. This is only one of them. I've got a lot more here. All forgeries. He made quite a nice bit out of it, anyway. He thinks they're all nicely burned. I saw him burn them. But when he knows we've got these, what can he do? He'll have to pay. It's a bit of cake, didn't I tell you? He'll have to pay. Just you put in anything, Mr Thursby. You won't need my help – any lawyer's jargon will do.'

'D'you call blackmail lawyer's jargon?' asked Roger.

'Now,' said Mr Streak, 'don't misunderstand me. I only want my fair share.'

'Your fair share, I should imagine,' said Roger, 'would be about five years, and I sincerely hope you get it one day. I'm sorry, Mr Glade, but I'm not surprised I couldn't understand these instructions. Perhaps you wouldn't mind taking Mr Streak away.'

'I'm so sorry about this' said Mr Glade. 'I'd no idea.'

'Of course you hadn't,' said Roger, 'but let's get rid of Mr Streak, shall we?'

As they left Roger's chambers, Mr Streak said to Mr Glade. 'But I don't understand. What did I do wrong, old boy?'

Roger sent for Donald. 'Who are Glade and Bream?' he asked. 'D'you know anything about them? I don't remember seeing them before.'

'No,' said Donald, 'they're new. All right, aren't they?'

'They may be, but their client isn't. I think you'd better give them a miss in future.'

'O.K., sir. Oh – you know you're going down to Westlea on Friday? I'm sorry . . . I couldn't get out of it. I did all I could.'

'Oh, that's all right,' said Roger. 'It'll be a change to go to a police court again.'

'A Magistrate's Court,' said Donald.

'Sorry,' said Roger. 'They were called police courts when I first heard of them.'

'Well, I'm glad you're not annoyed,' said Donald. 'I didn't expect you to take it so calmly.'

'Oh, well,' said Roger – but he blushed.

'Well, I'd got something to tell you to make up for it, but I needn't have troubled,' said Donald.

'Oh?'

'You'll have company on the way. Who d'you think they've taken in to lead for the prosecution?'

'Not Henry?'

'Right first time. Pity you can't settle it. That's the trouble about crime. It has to go all the way.'

'This one may not,' said Roger. 'It's out of the usual run.'

'No?' said Donald.

'Yes,' said Roger.

'Trust you to do a wangle,' said Donald. 'Blast,' he added suddenly.

'What's up?'

'It doesn't matter. I forgot to back something in the one o'clock. Wangle reminded me of it. But look, sir, I tell you what. You're going to Westlea on Friday. The Annington meeting's on Saturday. Why not make a week-end of it? I'll run Conference in the three-thirty. I wasn't going to, but I will if you'll come. You've never been to a race meeting, have you?'

'Only once,' said Roger. 'It doesn't sound at all a bad idea. A week-end at Westlea. I've got a friend there, as a matter of fact. She might join us.'

'Now I understand,' said Donald. 'Never known you take a brief out of town like that before.'

Chapter 13

CRABTREE IN CHARGE?

─────

HENRY and Roger drove together to Westlea in Roger's car on the day fixed for the magisterial hearing. Sally was to join them the next day.

'This is a comic outing,' said Henry on the way. 'The prosecution and defence conspiring together to do down a couple of prosecution witnesses.'

'What troubles me a bit,' said Roger, 'is my cross-examination. It's been suggested by your people that I should cross-examine the inspector and sergeant on what they would expect to be Glacier's story – i.e., that no money passed. Well – I don't quite see how I can do that even if you agree to it, as no doubt you would.'

'Why not?'

'It doesn't seem to me that I can put to a witness who's giving evidence on oath what I know to be a false case—even with the concurrence of the prosecution. How can I properly invite a witness to swear to something which I know to be untrue? Suppose I say – "I suggest to you that no money passed between you and Mr Glacier," and suppose he agreed with me – after all it's my object to persuade him to do so – surely I'd be a party to his perjury? That can't be right.'

'I see your point,' said Henry. 'Not being as scrupulous as you are, I confess I hadn't thought of it before. But you're obviously right. You can't.'

'Of course I don't have to cross-examine at all – or I can just play about with them for a bit without putting my case to them. But either I must put my case to them or just ask them about their case. I can't put a false case to them.'

'Right as usual,' said Henry. 'What a lot Grimeyboy taught you.'

'It was by example then,' said Roger. 'You supplied the words.'

'Yes, I'm quite good at supplying words,' said Henry, 'if I don't have to look them up. Well, that's settled then. I'll explain why you're not doing what was suggested. With regard to the rest, it'll just go its normal course, I suppose. I gather your client's pockets are going to be stuffed full of one-pound notes, all marked. I can never make out why they have to mark them as well as take the numbers. I'm looking forward to meeting your Anne.'

'I hope you'll like her. I don't really know her very well myself yet.'

'But looking forward to doing so, I gather.'

'Very much.'

'I seem to sense much the same happening to you as happened to me when I met your Sally.'

'Stranger things have happened.'

'Good. I gather Donald's going to take us all to the races. He's a very important person on a racecourse. He goes in by the "Owners and Trainers Only". We just go where we're told. I like these small meetings. They're much nearer to point-to-points. Friendly atmosphere about the place and not so many toughs from London.'

'We represent the toughs from London this time.'

Eventually they reached the Westlea Court. Mr Plumb and Mr and Mrs Glacier were already there, and Roger joined them outside the Court. Henry met his junior – a Treasury junior named Digby – and the representative from the Director of Public Prosecutions who was instructing him. The Bench consisted of Mr Bragge, who kept a large grocery store, Mrs Thwaites, who had once represented the town as a Member of Parliament, the Chairman, Sir Henry Carstairs, who owned most of the land in the neighbourhood and had once read for the Bar, Mr Pantin, who was on the point of retiring because of old age, and Dr Spicer, who was a retired local doctor. They were already sitting, but the Glaciers' case was timed to come on later. Roger and Henry went into Court to see how matters were progressing. They arrived in time to hear Crabtree cross-examining a police surgeon. Crabtree's client was accused of being in charge of a car while under the influence of drink.

'Now, doctor,' said Crabtree, 'I don't want there to be any mistake about this. You've said that the defendant was unable to pass three out of four tests through which you put him; well, it all depends upon what you mean by pass, doesn't it? Some people might think differently, mightn't they – no, doctor, that wasn't the question, what I want to ask you is this – first of all you smelled the defendant's breath and you say it smelled of alcohol; isn't it true that if you have any alcohol, however little, you smell of it – unless you've taken cloves or something, and would it surprise you to learn that my client always carries some cloves with him – his wife you know – you understand what I mean, doctor – well, if the defendant had wanted to deceive you, he could have taken one first, couldn't he –'

The doctor, having spotted the actual question, jumped in with an answer before Crabtree could continue. 'Certainly, if he'd been sober enough to think of it.'

'Really, doctor, don't you think that's rather offensive. I mean –' But the doctor, who enjoyed family games, suddenly thought of a new one – Get in with your answer. Perhaps he might suggest it to the B.B.C.

'Not in the least offensive,' he replied. 'You said yourself he deceives his wife that way.'

'Is that your answer?' said Crabtree. The doctor waited for a moment. It didn't seem possible. He was not aware that Crabtree's question was what may be termed a marking-time catch-phrase frequently used by some counsel when they are caught on the wrong foot by a witness. As Crabtree remained strangely silent, the doctor eventually answered.

'Yes, it is.'

'I see,' said Crabtree.

'Good,' said the doctor.

The Chairman decided to intervene in the rather uneven

contest, and metaphorically told the doctor to stand away from Crabtree until he'd risen to his feet.

'I think,' he said, 'you should confine your remarks to answering questions, doctor.'

'I'm only too pleased,' said the doctor, 'when I can find one.'

'That'll do, doctor,' said the Chairman, administering a caution to the rather too lively doctor, who was apparently so full of fight that he was prepared to challenge the referee.

'Now,' said Crabtree, 'you complain that the defendant's tongue was furry, well what I want to know is, don't lots of people have furry tongues? Look at the medicines advertised – my tongue used to be like this – picture of an ermine coat – now it is like this – picture of a sirloin of beef – you know the sort of thing, well –'

'I've never seen that particular advertisement,' said the doctor. 'I think it's rather good. Which particular medicine does it advertise?'

Crabtree and the Chairman came in together. 'Don't ask me/him questions. You're there to answer mine/his.'

'Sorry, your Worships,' said the doctor, 'it slipped out. I'm sorry, Mr Crabtree.'

'Thank you,' said Crabtree.

'Thank *you*,' said the doctor.

'Next question,' said the Chairman. He felt that if he didn't get the doctor out of the box soon the proceedings might get out of hand.

'Now, doctor,' said Crabtree, 'you could only examine his tongue if he put it out, or at any rate if he opened his mouth –'

'Correct,' said the doctor. 'Full marks.'

'Dr Bulstrode,' said the Chairman, 'this is not your consulting-room, nor a music hall. Please behave yourself. You're in a court of law.'

'Well, unless you forced his jaws open – and I assume you didn't do that . . . well, unless you forced –'

'No, I didn't do that,' slipped in the doctor, and added – to himself – 'I was a bit late that time.'

'Unless you forced his jaws open and you say you didn't do that, then you must have asked him to open his mouth and put out his tongue, and he must have done so – now, doctor –'

'I know what you're going to say,' said the doctor. 'Well, I'm –'

'Will you kindly wait till I've formulated the question, doctor,' thundered Crabtree. 'This is really too bad. The question I was going to ask you was this – if he did what you told him or, if you prefer it, what you asked him – if he did that –'

'He must have understood what I said and complied with my request? I take it that is your question,' said the doctor.

'Yes,' said Crabtree, a little crestfallen.

'That's all right,' said the doctor encouragingly. 'I thought it would save a little time if I answered before you asked it. And the answer is – he was not blind drunk or unconscious – he was just wholly unfit to be in charge of a car.'

'That was not the question I asked you,' said Crabtree.

'I thought it was what the case was about,' said the doctor. 'I'm sorry if it wasn't the answer you wanted.'

Roger whispered to Henry. 'This is going to go on all day at this rate.'

'They've had one day already,' whispered Henry. 'I read about it. The chap was as drunk as an owl, but there's a nice point as to whether he was in charge. Why don't you say something to him?'

'You try,' said Roger. 'He'll take it from you.'

Henry worked his way into the seat next to Crabtree and, just after the doctor had floored him for quite a long count, he touched his arm :

'I say, old boy, why don't you let the "drunk" go, and stick to the "in charge"?'

'D'you really think so?' said Crabtree. 'I mean to say –'

'Yes,' said Henry. 'I've read about it; I think you've got a jolly good run on it, but the "drunk" is as dead as a doornail.'

'Thanks so much,' said Crabtree, rather relieved. 'No more questions, thank you, doctor.'

'But I haven't answered your last yet. I should like to.'

'Oh, very well,' said Crabtree.

'Would you mind repeating it?' said the doctor. It was what might be called a prize Crabtree, with hardly any beginning, no end and a sticky mess in the middle.'

'Certainly not,' snapped Crabtree.

'But how can I answer it if you don't?' complained the doctor.

'I didn't ask you to answer it,' said Crabtree.

'But you did, really you did,' said the doctor. 'It began with – now, doctor, I want you to answer this question categorically, yes or no – I remember as far as that – it's the rest I've forgotten.'

'Then how can you answer it?' said Crabtree, feeling that something was required of him.

'That's what I should like to know,' said the doctor.

The Chairman intervened.

'Thank you, doctor,' he said. 'You may stand down. Is that the case for the prosecution?' he added, looking at the solicitor for the police.

'Yes, your Worships.'

'Very well then. Now, Mr Crabtree, are you going to call any evidence?'

'Submit there's no evidence of "in charge",' said Henry.

'I submit', said Crabtree, 'that there's no evidence that my client was in charge of this car at the material time.'

'That's an interesting point,' said the Chairman, 'and we shall need the help of both you and your opponent over it. But, if you call no evidence, we shall be bound to come to the conclusion that your client was under the influence of drink at the material time. At least that's my view on the evidence so far given. I don't know about my colleagues.' His colleagues nodded assent. 'It seems that we're agreed on that then,' said the Chairman. 'So it's up to you, Mr Crabtree.'

'I'm entitled, am I not,' said Crabtree, after a whispered

conversation with Henry, 'to have a ruling on my submission before I elect whether to call evidence or not?'

'We'll consult our clerk about that,' said the Chairman. There was a whispered conversation between the clerk of the Court and the Chairman. After a few minutes the Chairman said :

'Very well, Mr Crabtree, we'll hear your submission.'

'If your Worships please,' said Crabtree. 'Now, your Worships, I submit that for a man to be in charge of a car he must be *in charge*, by which I mean that it's no good for the prosecution to prove that he *might* have been in charge. they must prove that he *was* in charge, and it's no good for them to prove that he was in charge *before* the material time or *after* the material time, they must prove he was in charge *at* the material time. Now, what are the facts? The car was owned by my client. That's admitted. But he had a paid driver driving him. How can he be said to be in charge?'

'It all depends what "in charge" means,' said the clerk. 'If you can tell your driver to drive fast or slow or to stop or to drive here or there, or not to drive at all and to hand over the wheel to you, who is in charge of the car? The driver may be driving it as long as you let him, but why aren't you in charge?'

'It would be ridiculous if that were the case,' said Crabtree. 'A man who knows he's unfit to drive gets someone else to drive him home – what harm has he done? What harm can he do?'

'He can tell the driver to stop and hand over the wheel,' said the clerk. 'And if it's his car, the driver would presumably have to obey him. The only other course open to the driver would be to drive to a policeman or to get out and find one. He surely couldn't legally refuse to stop driving. It would be a trespass, wouldn't it?'

'If what you say is right, then a drunken man is allowed to be driven in his own car even if he takes no part in the driving, just because he may wake up and order the driver out of the car?'

Crabtree's unusually intelligent and intelligible replies

were due to the fact that most of them were being pumped
into him by Henry, who was now taking a personal interest
in the case.

'Each case must depend on its own facts,' said the clerk.
'If the friend of a drunk man put him unconscious in his
own car and drove him home, the position might very well
be different. In such a case the owner of the car would not
even know he was in it. I should have thought that, to be
guilty of an offence while in charge of a car, a man must
know that he is in charge. There must at least be some evidence that he did know. Then again, I suppose, if a man
were too drunk to drive but could understand what was happening round about him, he could license someone else to
drive on the express term that he could not determine the
licence until he had been deposited at his home. I suppose
in such a case you could say that the owner could not law-
fully terminate the licence and order the driver out of the
car until the journey home was over. In such a case it might
well be said that the owner was not in charge. He would
have temporarily parted with his right to be in charge.'

'If that can be done expressly,' whispered Henry, 'it can
be done impliedly.'

Crabtree passed on the observation.

'I agree,' said the Chairman, 'but is that the case here?
Let us consider the evidence. Your client had a paid driver.
The driver in backing the car from behind another had a
very slight accident and damaged a wing. Your client said :
"Here, give me the ruddy key. You can't drive. You're
drunk." At that moment – very fortunately – a policeman
arrived. "Who's in charge of this car?" he asked. "He is,"
said the chauffeur, who was still angry at being told off. "Is
that right?" asked the policeman. "He's my ruddy driver,"
said your client, "but he's not fit to drive. He's drunk." The
evidence was that the driver was completely sober and that
it was your client, if anyone, who was under the influence
of drink.'

'The fact that he said his driver wasn't fit to drive didn't
necessarily imply that he was going to drive himself. He

might have been going for the police,' whispered Henry. Crabtree repeated it.

'And the statement made by the driver wasn't admitted by the defendant to be true. On the contrary, he said "He's the driver,"' went on Henry, followed by Crabtree.

'This case,' said the clerk, quite genially, 'seems to be involving a certain amount of outside professional interest.'

'We welcome such interest,' said the Chairman, who was profoundly grateful for Henry's assistance. 'Tell me, Mr Crabtree,' he went on, looking at Henry, 'do you say that a car need not be in the charge of anyone?'

Henry nodded.

'I do,' said Crabtree.

'If I leave my car on the highway, who is in charge of it while I'm away?'

Henry shrugged his shoulders, which was correctly translated by Crabtree into : 'It depends on the circumstances.'

Henry whispered to Crabtree, and a moment later Crabtree said : 'My client did not drive, he did not try to drive, he merely tried to prevent someone whom he thought unfit to drive from driving.'

'Well, Mr Crabtree,' said the Chairman, 'I think we'd like to hear what your opponent has to say.'

'A good deal,' said a small solicitor with a fiery red moustache. 'It will, in my submission,' he went on, 'be an encouragement to drunken drivers in the neighbourhood if the Bench finds there is no case to answer here. Here is a man obviously under the influence of drink who says to his driver, "Give me the keys." What for? To drive, of course.'

'Why not simply to stop the driver from driving?' asked the Chairman.

'Because someone has to drive the car!'

'Why?'

'To get home. Theoretically, I agree, the request to hand over the keys could be merely to stop the man from driving, but from the practical point of view what did it really mean? "Here, give me the keys."'

'May it not have depended on the emphasis?' asked the

clerk. 'If he said – 'here give *me* the keys' – that might suggest that he was going to drive. But if he said "here *give* me the keys" that could simply mean he was going to stop him driving. I confess my note does not show where the emphasis was placed. I don't know if any of their Worships remembers.'

Their Worships did not. At the time the question was asked the possible importance of the emphasis was not apparent to anyone.

'I suppose we might ask him again,' queried the Chairman.

'But he's heard all this argument,' said the clerk.

'I don't see why that should make any different,' said the prosecuting solicitor.

'I object,' said Crabtree. 'He has shown obvious bias against my client from the start, by which I mean that throughout his evidence –'

'We quite understand, Mr Crabtree,' said the Chairman. 'You object.'

'Yes.'

'All the same, unless my colleagues disagree, I think I'd like to hear the witness again.'

The driver was recalled. The clerk reminded him that he was still under oath.

'Perhaps I'd better ask the question,' said the clerk.

'Yes, please,' said the Chairman.

'Mr Mills,' said the clerk, 'would you repeat to the Bench please what the defendant said to you after you'd bumped the wing.'

'It wasn't my fault,' said the witness.

'Never mind about that,' said the clerk. 'What did the defendant say immediately afterwards?'

'He said : "Let's have the ruddy keys. You're drunk." '

'I thought you said that he said "Here, give me the ruddy keys." '

'So he did.'

'But you've just said he said "Let's have the ruddy keys." '

'So he did.'

'It can't have been both – or was it perhaps both?'

'I don't understand.'

'Did he say "Let's have the ruddy keys"?'

'Yes.'

'Did he say anything else?'

'Yes. "You're drunk." '

'Anything else?'

'No.'

'Then he didn't say,' went on the clerk, ' "Here give me the ruddy keys." '

'Yes he did. I've just told you so.'

'You've told us that he said "Let's have the ruddy keys." '

'That's right.'

'And that he said nothing else except "You're drunk." '

'That's right.'

'Then he didn't say "Here give me the ruddy keys." '

'I tell you, he did.'

'But "here give me the keys" isn't the same as "let's have the keys." '

The witness looked blank.

'Well?' said the clerk.

'Well what?' asked the witness.

'They're not the same, are they? They're different words.'

'I don't remember the *words* he said, only just *what* he said.'

The clerk turned to the Chairman.

'We shan't get any further than that, I'm afraid, your Worship,' he said.

'I should like to ask him some questions,' said Crabtree.

'I shouldn't,' whispered Henry.

'Very well, Mr Crabtree, what is your question?'

'I've changed my mind,' said Crabtree. 'No questions.' There was a whisper from Henry.

'But I should like to submit,' said Crabtree, 'that that evidence strengthens my submission. It shows that the sense of what the defendant said was that he wanted to prevent his driver from driving.'

'Well, what do you say, Mr Mountain?' the Chairman

said to the prosecuting solicitor. 'You surely have to prove that the defendant was in charge of the car when the police arrested him – not just that it is possible that if the police had come a little later he might then have been in charge.'

'That is true, your Worship,' said the solicitor, 'but I submit there is at least evidence on which the Bench could decide that the defendant was in charge.'

'You have to prove your case,' said the Chairman.

'Not at the moment, with respect, your Worship. I only have to show that there is a case for the defendant to answer.'

'Surely,' said the Chairman, 'if at this stage we think the prosecution has not proved its case we can say so. A jury can stop the case after the evidence for the prosecution is over, can't they? If they can, why can't we? I'll ask the clerk if you like.'

He talked for a few minutes to the clerk. At the end he said : 'Thank you very much. I'm not sure that I'm very much the wiser – no offence to the learned clerk. I still think that, if my colleagues and I are not satisfied that the defendant was in charge of the car when he was arrested, the case ought to be dismissed.'

His colleagues nodded.

'Anything more to say, Mr Mountain?'

'It doesn't seem much use, your Worship.'

'No, I don't think it would be. Let the defendant stand up.'

A red-faced man stood up from where he had been sitting in front of the dock. 'Luke Halliday,' said the Chairman, 'we do not wish our decision in this case to encourage drivers of vehicles to think that they can drink with impunity. On the contrary, this Bench takes a very severe view indeed of drivers who are found guilty of being drunk while in charge of a vehicle. Only a few weeks ago we suspended such a man's licence for seven years. We shall not hesitate to do the same again. Let no one think that drunken, wanton, or even merely bad driving can take place in this area without the guilty party being in grave peril of fine, prison and, perhaps most important of all, of losing his licence. But in every case the prosecution has to satisfy us by evidence that the offence has been committed. In the present case we are not satisfied on the evidence that you were in charge of the car when you were arrested. The case is dismissed.' The red-faced man stood still for a moment, swaying slightly; then he spoke.

'How much?' he asked before he was led away to have it explained to him by his friends.

'I thought you did that very well,' said Roger to Henry. 'We'd have still been there if you hadn't.'

In spite of Henry's intervention, however, their case could not start until after lunch. Before they went off to the Glorious, Roger saw Mr Glacier and Mr Plumb.

'I have arranged a magnificent lunch for you,' said Mr Glacier. 'I hope you will all enjoy it, particularly your – how do you call him? – your opposite number. Perhaps when he comes to cross-examine me you might remind him that the *Sauce béarnaise* was specially made for him. Or does that too come under the Corruption Act?'

'It would if I weren't taking him to lunch,' said Roger. 'But tell me something much more important. What's happened so far?'

'As I have already told the good Mr Plumb,' said Mr Glacier, 'my pockets are – how do you say? – stuffed with notes – not this time taken from my safe – but from the public purse. I am to seek an opportunity of an interview with either the sergeant or the inspector. And then I have my instructions. I shall do it in much the same way as it is stated that I did it before.'

'Have you spoken to either of them yet?' asked Mr Plumb.

'No,' said Mr Glacier, 'I do not wish to be too – too obvious about it. I am learning, you see.'

'D'you know,' said Mr Plumb, 'that there are about thirty detectives inside and outside the Court, all watching the inspector and sergeant like hawks?'

'How lucky,' said Mr Glacier, 'that telepathy has not been

brought up to modern standards of efficiency. When it is –
when by a machine I can transfer my thoughts to you –
when you by a machine can suck my thoughts from
me – then I think the time will have come to go to one of
the other planets. Let us hope that there will be a regular
service by then. I cannot think of anything worse than that
people can know what I am really thinking. Then the word
truth would disappear. There would unfortunately be nothing else. How boring. But I am detaining you. Please make
the fullest use of the hotel services.'

Chapter 14

INTRODUCING MR TRENT

'I SHALL have a sherry,' said Henry. 'I suppose you'll stick to tomato juice, Roger.'

'Thanks,' said Roger. 'Must keep awake somehow during your opening.'

'Why bother?' said Henry. 'Ah, here are our clients. I'm sure they'll be sociable and join me. Mr Lockwood, sherry for you? Mr Plumb?'

Mr Lockwood, the representative from the Director of Public Prosecutions, said that a sherry would be very nice. Mr Plumb, in his usual mournful tones, agreed and had nothing to add.

'I gather my junior's had to go off somewhere else,' said Henry.

'He's left a pupil to represent him,' said Roger. 'A young man called Trent. Rather reminds me of myself. To look at, I mean. Hope he's not quite such an ass.'

'Where is he?' said Henry.

'I told him to be here,' said Roger. 'Perhaps he's in the lounge. I'll go and look.'

'Why should you look for my junior's pupils?' said Henry. 'I'll go.'

'You needn't,' said Roger. 'Here he is.'

Anthony Trent, aged twenty-three, bespectacled, arrived. 'I hope I'm not late,' he said in a rather fruity voice, which, like his appearance, seemed older than he was. 'Good of you to ask me,' he added. Roger glanced at Henry.

'Nice of you to come,' said Henry.

'I suppose I should be here really,' said Mr Trent, 'as I'm the sole personal representative of Digby. I think he's awfully good, you know,' he added.

'I'm sure he'd be very pleased to hear you say that,' said Henry.

'Now you're pulling my leg,' said Mr Trent.

'I wouldn't take such a liberty,' said Henry.

'What I like about the Bar,' said Mr Trent, 'is the fact that as soon as you're called you're equal with everyone else. People who didn't know would be amazed if they heard me call you, a silk of some standing –'

'Thank you,' interjected Henry.

'If they heard me call you just Blagrove. They'd think I was being uppish.'

'Extraordinary, isn't it?' said Roger.

'Which reminds me,' said Mr Trent. 'This is a most extraordinary case. But there was one point I thought I ought to mention to you, Blagrove. It's this –'

'D'you think it'll keep till after lunch?' said Henry.

'Certainly, if you'd prefer it. But it is rather important. As a matter of fact, I think that everyone's missed it so far. You see, under the Prevention of Corruption Act, 1906 –'

'If you don't mind, we will wait,' said Henry. 'And, don't forget, our opponents are here in force.'

'Oh – it wouldn't matter their hearing,' said Mr Trent. 'It's a point which both sides appear not to have noticed.'

'And it's been left to – now, I quite forget your name,' said Henry.

'Trent. Tony Trent.'

'It's been left to Tony Trent to discover it.'

'Now you're pulling my leg again. I wasn't born yesterday, you know.'

'When were you called?' asked Roger.

'Ah,' said Mr Trent. 'That wasn't yesterday either. Three months ago, as a matter of fact. It's amazing what one can pick up in a short time.'

'Have you ever attended a conference with your lord and master?' asked Roger.

'I have, as a matter of fact,' said Mr Trent.

'Just one, I imagine,' said Roger.

Mr Trent looked mystified.

'You're quite right,' he said. 'But I expect there'll be another soon.'

'I shouldn't count on it,' said Roger. 'Did you happen to say anything yourself at the first conference?'

'Well, as a matter of fact, I did just point out something they didn't seem to have noticed.'

'They must have been pleased,' said Roger.

'Well, to be quite frank,' said Mr Trent, 'I wasn't sure if they were.'

'Didn't they thank you?' asked Henry.

'Well, not exactly.'

'Shocking,' said Henry.

'There you go again,' said Mr Trent.

'Suppose we go and have lunch,' said Henry.

'I'll join you in a moment,' said Roger. 'I've just seen —' and, without finishing the sentence, he left the bar. He caught Anne in the lounge.

'Hullo,' he said.

'Hullo.'

'It is nice to see you.'

'And you too.'

'Look, will you come to the races with us tomorrow? My clerk's got a horse running. It'll be a sort of chambers party. I'd like you to meet them — that's if you care to at all.'

'I should simply love it.'

'That's a sweet little hat.'

'I'm so glad you like it. Shall I wear it tomorrow?'

'Please.'

A pause.

'I'm afraid I must go now. I've got this case on.'

'Yes, of course. Father's very worried about it.'

'I like your father.'

'I think he likes you.'

'Does he? Does he really?'

'Yes — I'm sure he does.'

'I am glad.'

A pause.

'And you?'

She nodded. 'I must go now. Where shall I meet you tomorrow?'

'Shall I call for you? We'll lunch at the course. About twelve do?'

'Lovely.'

'I'm so glad you can come.'

'So am I.'

'I must go now.'

'So must I.'

'Must you really?'

'Yes, really.'

'I should like to stay here talking to you instead of having lunch.'

'So would I.'

'Would you really?'

'But we can't. Anyway, it would look silly.'

'I suppose it would. But I shouldn't mind.'

'Nor should I really.'

'Wouldn't you really?'

'No, not really.'

'Really?'

'Really.'

'Darling,' said Roger, and hurried off to lunch. He found Mr Trent holding forth on the virtues and vices of some of the judges and silks he had come across in his three months' career.

'Now I think Swallow's really good,' he was saying. 'There's a top-class lawyer, if you like.'

'How d'you recognize one?' asked Roger.

'Oh – you can tell in no time,' said Mr Trent.

'I wish I could,' said Henry. 'You must teach me some time.'

'Now,' said Mr Trent, wagging his finger playfully at Henry.

'I don't know if it's the lobster cocktail,' said Henry, 'but I'm not sure that I don't feel a bit sick.'

'If it is,' said Mr Trent, 'you'd have a marvellous action for damages. We'd all be witnesses. Of course Thursby's client wouldn't have to pay. They're all insured, you know.'

'Is that really so?' asked Roger.

'Oh, yes,' said Mr Trent. 'You see, with all the possible claims by the public, all these places are insured.'

'I think, Henry,' said Roger, 'that we ought to find that out before you actually make a claim. I'm sure you wouldn't like my client to be out of pocket over it.'

'But you can really take my word for it,' said Mr Trent, 'they're all insured. It would be quite extraordinary if he weren't.'

'But extraordinary things do happen,' said Roger. 'Let me see,' he added, 'when did you say you were born – I mean called?'

'Just three months ago to the day. Exactly twelve years five months after you. I've turned you up in the Law List. I suppose you'll be taking silk soon. Blagrove took it three years ago. I like to know these things.'

'I wonder you find time to look in the Law List with all the other things you do,' said Henry.

Mr Trent smiled and waved his finger at him. Roger shuddered.

Mr and Mrs Glacier kept well out of the way during lunch. Usually they had a table in the restaurant so that they could keep an eye on things. This time they lunched in their private room. But the food they ordered for their legal guests was really superb. If only it had been dinner, thought Roger, I might have been able to do justice to it. I wish tomorrow would come.

Chapter 15

THE GLACIER CASE BEGINS

'May it please your Worships,' said Henry, opening the case for the prosecution, 'I appear in this case with my learned friend Mr Digby, and my learned friend Mr Thursby appears for the defendants.'

Henry found someone pulling his coat. It was Mr Trent trying to remind him that he was representing Digby and that Henry ought to say either that he was appearing with his learned friend Mr Trent or at least with his learned friends Mr Digby and Mr Trent.

'Now look,' said Henry, turning to Mr Trent. 'Please keep your mouth shut throughout the whole of this case and leave me alone. If you can't be quiet, go and play in the street. And I'm not pulling your leg,' he added.

Mr Trent retired hurt for a moment. 'And I thought he was such a nice chap,' he said to himself. 'But I don't expect he means it. I suppose he's a bit nervous at the beginning of a case. That must be it. I'll help him by showing that I don't mind.'

'That's all right, Blagrove,' he whispered. 'But if you want my help, I'm here.'

'Shut up,' said Henry.

'The defendants in this case,' he went on, addressing the Bench, 'are the proprietors of the Glorious Hotel of this town; and this case arises out of a prosecution in respect of certain breaches of the licensing laws which are alleged to have occurred at that hotel and for which it is alleged that the two defendants are responsible. I should say at the outset that for the purposes of this case it does not matter one way or the other whether the defendants or either of them are guilty of those offences or not. I am quite prepared to assume that they are not guilty. The only material fact is that they were in fact served with summonses charging them with licensing offences.' Henry then went on to explain to the Bench in some detail the facts as alleged by the prosecution. It had been agreed between the prosecution and defence to prolong the proceedings sufficiently to ensure that there would be another day's hearing in the Magistrate's Court. This was in order to have an interval before the magistrates committed for trial, during which the Glaciers would have a further opportunity of trying to bribe the inspector and sergeant. Should the plot prove successful, the prosecution against the Glaciers would be withdrawn before committal. Accordingly Henry took up a rather longer time in opening the case than he would normally have taken. When he had finished he called as his first witness the inspector – Inspector Worcester. After the usual preliminary questions, Henry asked him about the licensing prosecution and finally asked him to deal with the interview when the money was handed to him. The inspector cleared his throat.

'On the 14th December last, in company with Sergeant Warwick of the Carpshire County Police, I called on the defendants at the Glorious Hotel. I was shown into their private office. Both Mr and Mrs Glacier were there. I formally asked them their names. They were in fact well known to me. I then said "I'm afraid I have to serve you each with these summonses", and I handed them each two summonses.'

'I call for the original summonses served,' said Henry. Roger handed them to Henry and the usher took them from him to the witness.

'These are the four summonses,' went on Inspector Worcester. 'The first defendant read the summonses and then said –' The inspector referred to his notebook and was about to read out from it when Roger interposed with :

'How long after the interview were those notes made?'

'As soon as I returned to the police station,' said the inspector.

'All right?' said Henry.

'If you please,' said Roger.

'Go on, inspector,' said Henry. 'What did the first defendant say?'

'He said,' continued the inspector, ' "Is this really necessary?" I said : "I'm afraid it is." He said : "I really don't see why. There's a perfectly good explanation." I said : "You will be able to tell that to the magistrates." He said : "But I don't like the idea of appearing in Court. The publicity's bad for the hotel." I said : "I'm very sorry. There is no alternative." He said : "But surely there are ways of – how do you say? – of arranging these things?" I said : "I don't know of any and what do you mean by 'arranging these things' ?" He said : "Oh – you know the sort of thing I mean, inspector, surely?" I said : "I certainly don't?" He then went to a safe in his room. I said : "What are you doing?" He said : "I'll tell you in a moment." Very soon afterwards he came back from the safe with a bundle of notes in his hands. I said : "What are those for?" He said : "To pay the fine, of course." I said : "you haven't been fined yet and, in any event, you can't pay it now." He said : "There are countries where people get fined on the spot for some things." I said : "This is not one of them." He said : "Don't these cases take a great deal of your time when you could be doing something more valuable?" I said : "They're my duty like everything else. If it isn't one thing, it's another." He said : "Well, you'd do much better catching murderers and bank robbers and even some of the motorists who kill five thousand people every year." I said : "I do the cases that come into my hands, whatever they are, and this is one of them." He said : "If we're convicted how much d'you think we'll be fined?" I said : "That's a matter for the Bench. I can't discuss it with you." He said : "Well, it wouldn't be much for a first offence – particularly if you give us a good character." I said : "I know nothing whatever against you." That was true, your Worships.'

'I hope it's all meant to be true,' intervened Roger.

'I hope my learned friend will behave himself,' said Henry. 'Go on, inspector.'

'He then said: "Look, the fine wouldn't be more than this, would it?" and handed me the bundle of notes he was holding. They were one-pound Treasury notes, your Worships. I said: "I've told you I don't know what it will be." He said: "Well, keep them on account. You can give me back the change later." I said: "I can't do anything like that." He said: "Why not? Is it another of these red tapes I hear so much of?" I said: "It isn't a question of red tape. I've told you already that you haven't been fined and that, if you are, I don't know how much it will be. Whatever it is must be paid to the Court and not to me." He said: "Well, keep it anyway. I've plenty more." I then suspected that he might be trying to bribe me.'

'No!' said Roger.

'I really must ask my learned friend to refrain from these offensive and unnecessary interruptions,' said Henry. 'They serve no proper purpose and they are discourteous to the Bench, to the witness and to me.'

'I say,' Roger murmured faintly, so that only Henry could hear.

'Go on, inspector,' said Henry.

'My subsequent actions were based upon my belief that the defendant was endeavouring to commit an offence against the Prevention of Corruption Act 1906. I then said to the defendant: "What is this money for?" He said: "For you and the sergeant." I said: "What d'you expect for it?" He said: "Whatever I can get. If you can stop the summonses there's some more waiting for you. If you can't, you can make the evidence as friendly as possible." I said: "Very well. Thank you. I'll see what can be done." He said: "That's better. I thought you'd be sensible in the end. I suppose I went at it rather clumsily." I then said: "Yes, we do like it wrapped up a bit more." He said: "All right, inspector, if you get me out of this I'll wrap up the same amount again and a bit more." I said: "Thank you." Shortly afterwards the sergeant and I left. We went straight to the police station and saw Superintendent Rutland. I made a statement to him and handed him the notes. In my presence he placed them in an envelope which he then sealed with sealing wax and both he and I signed our names on it.'

'Is this the envelope?' asked Henry, and an envelope was handed to the witness.

'It is,' said the inspector.

'How many notes are there inside it?' asked Henry.

'Twenty,' said the inspector.

'Perhaps your Worships would care to open the envelope and a note can be made that it was opened in this court.'

'I think perhaps I'd better open it,' said the clerk. 'I could then give evidence of it later if necessary.'

'If you please,' said Henry.

'Any objection, Mr Thursby?' asked the Chairman.

'None, your Worship,' said Roger.

The clerk opened the envelope and counted out twenty one-pound notes.

'What happened next?' asked Henry.

'Acting on instructions from the superintendent, I called again on the defendants and again saw them in their office. Sergeant Warwick was with me. This was on the 27th December last. The following conversation then took place. He said : "Well, inspector, have you any good news for me?" I said : "I may have." He said : "Good. What's holding it up?" I said : "There are formalities, you know." He said : "Of course – everything here is formalities. How long will they take?" I said : "Well, I might be able to get it done in a week." "What's holding you back?" he asked. I just said : "Well –" and then he said : "Oh, of course, I see. It's I who am the slow one this time." He then went to the safe again and got out a bundle of notes. He came back from the safe and handed me the notes, saying : "I suppose you'll see the sergeant all right." I said : "Of course." He said : "You'll find twenty-five pounds there. I hope you think that's all right." I said : "Thank you, sir." The first defendant then said : "I can be sure this'll be the end of the matter?" I said : "You leave it to us, sir." We left shortly afterwards and I went straight to the superintendent again. I handed him the notes. They were placed in an envelope and sealed with sealing wax and both the superintendent and I signed the envelope.'

'Is this the envelope?' asked Henry. And the same procedure was adopted with the second envelope. This one was found to contain twenty-five notes. After this had been done the inspector continued his evidence.

'Later, after the summonses in this case had been issued, I went with Superintendent Rutland to serve them on the defendants. We saw both defendants in the same office as before. The superintendent told the defendants the nature of our visit and handed each of them summonses. The second defendant said nothing. The first defendant then looked hard at me and said : "This is infamous." The superintendent then cautioned him and the first defendant said : "I shall see my solicitor about this – it is infamous."'

'Tell me, inspector,' said Henry, 'what part did Mrs Glacier play at these three interviews?'

'She said nothing that I remember,' said the inspector.

'What was she doing when the first defendant was saying what you have told us?'

'She was standing or sitting next to him.'

'But what was she doing? Was she reading or knitting or what?'

'She wasn't doing anything,' said the inspector.

'Could she hear what was said?'

'She could not have failed to do so,' said the inspector. 'Oh ... and I did forget to mention that the first time the male defendant went to the safe he could not find his keys, and the female defendant looked in her bag and handed them to him.'

'Did she say anything?'

'Not that I can remember. She may have said : "Oh, here they are," but I'm not at all sure.'

'Two of the summonses had been handed to her?'

'Yes.'

'Charging her with licensing offences?'

'Yes.'

'When Mr Glacier was saying what you've told us, did Mrs Glacier do or say anything to show that she disapproved of what he was doing?'

'Nothing at all.'

'If what you say is true, the first defendant was asking you to procure the withdrawal of all four summonses –'

'I wish my learned friend wouldn't lead,' said Roger.

'He has already said it,' said Henry.

'With respect he has not,' said Roger. 'At no time did the inspector say that the first defendant referred to four summonses.'

'He said the summonses,' said Henry, 'and that meant the four.'

'It might have meant the two served on him,' said Roger.

'What, and leave Mrs Glacier out in the cold?' said Henry.

'I know it's all very amusing,' said Roger, 'but this is a criminal prosecution and my clients are charged with a very serious offence. Both of them. I entirely agree with my learned friend that it may well be that if the defendant said what is alleged – which I do not accept for a moment – if he said that, he may well have been referring to the four summonses. My point is that my learned friend must not add anything to the evidence himself.'

'Very well,' said Henry, 'how many summonses had been served by you in respect of the alleged licensing offences?'

'Four,' said the inspector.

'What was the first defendant asking you to do?'

'To procure a withdrawal of the summonses.'

'Did he say that he only meant the two served on him?'

'He did not. He just referred to the summonses.'

'Did Mrs Glacier at any time by word or deed show that she thought Mr Glacier was not asking you to procure the withdrawal of the summonses against her?'

'No.'

'Or that she did not want her husband to pay you the money?'

'No, she did not. On the contrary, on the first occasion she gave him the keys of the safe.'

'Thank you, inspector,' said Henry.

Roger then got up.

'I want to make it plain,' he said, 'that I do not propose to cross-examine at length in this Court. Should the Bench find there is a case to answer against either defendant, my case will be fully put to the witnesses at the Assizes. I don't want there to be any doubt about that. Now, inspector, I think you've said you've known the defendants for some time?'

'Yes, sir. Perhaps three or four years.'

'And you know them to be persons of the highest character apart from these recent incidents?'

'Entirely, sir.'

'It must have surprised you when they offered you money in the manner you say they did?'

'It did, sir.'

'When did you first consider that an attempt was being made to corrupt you?'

'When he told me to keep the money.'

'Did you not suspect it before then?'

'Yes, sir, I suspected it.'

'When?'

'Well, sir, his whole attitude suggested something of the kind from the beginning but, of course, one sometimes jumps to conclusions too soon.'

'May I put it this way? Almost from the beginning you smelled something?'

'Yes, sir.'

'And when the scent was conclusive, you decided to trap him?'

'Yes, sir.'

'You must have found that very unpleasant.'

'Very, sir.'

'But you have to do these things.'

'Exactly, sir.'

'Mr Glacier obviously considered that what you did was infamous?'

'Yes, sir.'

'What do you think he considered infamous?'

'Leading him on, sir, I suppose – and then charging him.'

'So you led him on?'

'He didn't require much leading, sir.'

'I was only using your own words, inspector. You led him on?'

The inspector paused for a moment. 'Yes, sir, I suppose you may put it that way ... at a certain stage.'

'But it was you who put it that way, inspector. Let's not beat about the bush. From the moment you were satisfied he was trying to corrupt you and the sergeant, you led him on?'

'Yes, sir.'

'And lied to him in the process?'

'In accordance with my duty, sir.'

'Then the answer is yes, you lied to him?'

'At a certain stage, yes, sir.'

'How often do you lie to people to trap them into offences?'

'I didn't trap him into the offence, sir. He was already committing it. I merely had to obtain the evidence.'

'All right, I'll accept that for the moment. How often have you lied to people in order to obtain evidence?'

'I couldn't say, sir. Not often.'

'How often has anyone tried to bribe you before?'

'Only once, sir.'

'How long have you been in the force?'

'Twenty years, sir.'

'Starting as a uniformed constable?'

'Yes, sir.'

'D'you mean to say no one – not even a motorist – has ever – except on one occasion – expressly or impliedly tried to corrupt you?'

'There has only been one definite occasion apart from this, sir. I have had vague suggestions made before, but nothing definite enough to justify a prosecution.'

'I take it, then, that you've only been concerned in one prosecution for bribery before?'

'That is so, sir.'

'And is it right then that in no other case have you ever reported a case of bribery to your superior officer?'

'That is so, sir.'

'Have you done work in the West End of London?'

'Yes, sir.'

'There are some pretty undesirable types about there, are there not?'

'Yes, sir.'

'People who run disorderly houses and the like?'

'Yes, sir.'

'Have you been concerned in any prosecutions for that sort of offence?'

'Yes, sir.'

'How often?'

'I can't say exactly, sir. A number of times.'

'So many that you can't remember?'

'I wouldn't say that, sir, but on several occasions.'

'A dozen or more?'

'I don't think quite as many, sir.'

'Well, whatever the number, d'you mean to say that you were never offered anything by any of those gentry?'

'I was once, sir. That was the case I was referring to.'

'Well, that means that you were never offered anything by a motorist, a bookmaker, a barrow boy, or anyone else at any time in your career?'

'Not definitely, no, sir.'

'You must have moved in a very high class of undesirables.'

The inspector did not answer.

'At any rate,' continued Roger, without requiring an answer, 'you had to leave the motorists, barrow boys, bookmakers, and the scum of the West End and come to respectable people in Westlea before you had an honest-to-God case of bribery?'

'Except on the one occasion, that is so, sir.'

'A bit remarkable, isn't it?'

'I couldn't say, sir.'

'But you can, can't you, inspector? Take street book-makers and keepers of disorderly houses ... is it not within your knowledge that they often attempt to corrupt?'

'I have heard of cases, sir.'

'But only experienced one?'

'That is so, sir.'

'Now, let's come to another matter – Mrs Glacier. She never said anything you can remember except possibly "here they are" – referring to the keys?'

'That is so, sir.'

'She never offered you anything or gave you anything, did she?'

'No, sir.'

'When she offered the keys to her husband you didn't at that stage know that he was going to try to bribe you?'

'No, sir, not definitely. As I said, I was suspicious.'

'When he first handed you the money, you said that he said it was for the fine?'

'Yes, sir.'

'Well, at the time Mrs Glacier handed him the keys, there was no reason why she should not think that's what it was for?'

'I couldn't say, sir.'

'But you can, inspector. As far as you could see, had any-thing been said or done which showed Mrs Glacier that her husband was about to bribe you?'

'Nothing more than I've said, sir.'

'Well, then – even you, an experienced police officer, only suspected the possibility; can you suggest any reason why Mrs Glacier should even suspect that?'

'They might have discussed it before, sir.'

'Of course they *might*. Anything *might* have happened, but, as far as you can tell from what you saw and heard, they had not?'

'I couldn't say, sir, I certainly never heard them discuss it.'

'Didn't you really?' said Roger. 'Well, then, can you tell me why Mrs Glacier is charged at all?'

'That's not my responsibility,' said the inspector.

'But I presume you swore the information which led to the issue of the summonses?'

'That is true, sir, but it didn't rest with me who was to be charged. I simply swore to the facts, sir.'

'Are you opposed to her being charged, then?'

'Do you mean you want my personal views, sir?'

'What on earth have the inspector's personal views got to do with it?' interposed Henry. 'It will be for the Bench first, and later, if the defendants are committed, for the jury to express their personal views. I don't mind in the least what the inspector thinks. The object of evidence is to ascertain facts, not views.'

'Well,' said Roger, 'as my learned friend – and I don't blame him – feels so tender on this particular spot I won't aggravate the wound by pressing it.'

'I'm not in the least tender,' said Henry. 'If you like to ask me as representing the prosecution why Mrs Glacier is charged, I'll gladly tell you. All I object to is the wrong person being asked the question. The Director takes full responsibility for the charges in this case. I represent him, and I am the person to ask.'

'I can't cross-examine you,' said Roger.

'I shouldn't even mind that on this particular point,' said Henry. 'It's perfectly obvious why Mrs Glacier has been charged.'

'Not to the inspector,' said Roger.

'He hasn't been asked that,' said Henry.

'Well, I'll ask him,' said Roger.

'It's got nothing to do with him,' said Henry.

'I'm only trying to help,' said Roger. 'I gathered you wanted me to ask him.'

'Gentlemen,' interposed the Chairman, 'I'm sure you both know what's going on, but it's a little confusing for the Bench to have this altercation during the cross-examination of a witness. Do you think perhaps you could continue it outside the Court?'

'I was objecting to a question being asked by my learned

friend,' said Henry, 'and I'm afraid that unless my learned friend withdraws it, I shall have to trouble the Bench to rule on my submission.'

'But I thought Mr Thursby said he was not going to press the question,' said the Clerk.

'I did say that,' said Roger.

'Then I cannot think what the argument is about,' said the Chairman.

'Can you?' whispered Roger to Henry.

He continued to cross-examine the inspector for a further half hour, and then Sergeant Warwick was called. His evidence was substantially the same as that of the inspector. Roger cross-examined him slightly, but not as fully as the inspector.

That was as far as the Bench would go that day and the case was adjourned for a week. Outside the Court Mr Glacier came up to Roger and Mr Plumb. 'I must see you at once,' he said.

It transpired that he had taken an opportunity of speaking to the inspector when no one else appeared to be looking – though in fact they were under the observation of detectives the whole time – and asked him if he would see him. The inspector had given him an appointment at the police station for the following Monday.

'Mr Plumb,' said Roger, when they had learned this, 'you must go straight to the Chief Constable and tell him. Er – perhaps you'd like me to come too.'

They went straight to his house and waited till he returned.

'Right,' said Colonel Madderley, when they had told him. 'This is it. We'll have a microphone installed and, if he takes the money, we'll catch him with the notes on him when he comes out.'

'But he might say he was going straight to the superintendent with the money,' said Roger.

'Of course,' said the Chief Constable. 'Stupid of me. We must arrange for the superintendent to be the first person to see him when he comes out of the room.'

'And might I suggest, Chief Constable,' said Roger, 'that he makes an excuse for taking him into his office? Anything will do. A friendly chat or another case. Otherwise he could say he didn't want to discuss it in any place where they might be observed.'

'Another bull's-eye,' said the colonel. 'You've missed your vocation. It shall be done. I've been watching this particular fish for months. We'll see if we can get a rise out of him this time. That's in confidence, of course.'

Mr Plumb looked at Roger, who now had a very difficult decision to make. If it had been the first time the subject had been mentioned, he would have done what he had told Mr Plumb he ought to have done. But now the position was very different. Mr Plumb had already agreed to treat a similar statement in confidence. The colonel could rely on that promise to justify what was only a repetition of the statement. If Roger now stepped in and said it was not in confidence, the Chief Constable would not only be very annoyed but he might suspect double-dealing of some kind. On the other hand, if he simply said nothing he was, in effect, doing what Mr Plumb had already done. Silence in such a case must imply consent. If he was going to say at any later stage that the statement was not in confidence, he must say so now. It was all very difficult. In all the circumstances, he decided to do nothing, and he hoped more than ever that the inspector would be caught out and the prosecution of the Glaciers brought to an early end. He could foresee embarrassment and unpleasantness if this did not happen. And it did not help that he had already quite decided that, if she would have him, he was talking to his future father-in-law.

Chapter 16

STATISTICS

———

ROGER enjoyed the next day more than he had enjoyed anything for a long time. He put the affairs of Mr and Mrs Glacier out of his mind; he decided to forget that he would have to do a day and a half's work on Sunday and that, in addition to a vast amount of paper work, he had a difficult non-jury case first in the list on Monday. This shall be a *dies non* he said to himself – or rather it shall be a Dies with a capital D. To the races with Anne. True, chambers would be there in force, but he would be able to see her alone from time to time, and anyway he would be able to see her and be near to her. This is it. Thank heaven she can't drive a car or I'd never have met her. As he shaved he thought more and more about her. What a lovely name. What a lovely face. What a lovely voice. I wonder what Sally will think of her. I do hope she approves. She's nearly always right. Anyway, I can't help it if she doesn't.

He fetched her in his car and they met the others – Henry and Sally, Donald and his wife – in the restaurant in the members' enclosure. Donald had already drunk three quarters of a bottle of champagne laced with brandy.

'Hullo, Roger,' he said, 'I feel we're going to have a good day.' Roger introduced Anne and spoke for a few moments to Donald's wife.

'Two bottles of champagne,' said Donald to a waiter. 'No, make it a magnum. There's a feeling about a magnum like a thousand-guinea brief. This is going to be a party.'

It certainly was. They all drank champagne and brandy. Before lunch was over Roger found he was holding Anne's hand. He looked at Sally. He could tell at a glance that she approved. It was all right.

After lunch they went to the paddock and on the way

Sally took Roger by the arm out of earshot of the others. 'Well done,' she said.

'D'you mean it?'

'You know I do,' said Sally. 'I'm even a bit jealous. If you'd looked at me as you look at her I'd have been in heaven.'

'You make me feel most uncomfortable,' said Roger, 'I must have been awful. I think of myself sometimes and shiver. You're terribly happy with Henry, aren't you?'

'Who wouldn't be?' said Sally. 'I'm very lucky.'

'So am I – I hope,' said Roger. A sudden awful thought occurred to him . . . possibly he was assuming too much.

'You're all right,' said Sally, reading his thoughts. 'I saw the way she looked at you.'

'Hullo, Thursby,' said a voice. It was Mr Trent.

'Hullo,' said Roger, without much enthusiasm.

'I can give you something for the first race, if you like,' said Mr Trent. 'I know what I'm talking about.'

'That's very kind of you,' said Roger, 'but I don't know that we shall back anything in it.'

'Well, just in case,' said Mr Trent. 'Capsule. It's an outsider. But you'll see.'

'Thank you,' said Roger, and he and Sally moved on to catch up the others. They found them at the paddock. The horses in the first race were being led round. None of them looked very enthusiastic. Roger found Henry talking to another member of the Bar whom he knew slightly – Eagally.

'My dear chap,' Eagally was saying, 'I work it out on scientific principles. You just can't go wrong. What I mean is this. If a thing's always happened in the past it's going to happen in the future. That's fair enough, isn't it?'

'Very fair,' said Henry.

'Now, take this race;' said Eagally, looking at his race-card. 'There's a horse running that has never won a race. It's been out five times – not even placed. Now – and this is the point. This is a five-furlong race. I look at the breeding. I find that the sire was Fair Trial, a great sire of winners up to a mile. Now for the dam. The race-card tells you the name of the dam, but that's not enough. You want to know the name of the sire of the dam. I get that from here,' and he brought out a little book. 'You see, most racegoers are so stupid they don't know about this. Just imagine, the race-card itself – produced by people who are supposed to know about these things – not giving you the sire of the dam. But that's how things are. Now I find that the sire of this horse's dam was Panorama, one of the greatest sires of sprinters. So, on the one hand you have Fair Trial and the other Panor-ama. A perfect combination for a five-furlong race. But it isn't just that. I tell you, I go in for this scientifically. If you look up all the horses which have been sired by Fair Trial out of a dam by Panorama, you'll find that they all win races sooner or later and nearly always sooner.'

'Suppose,' said Roger, 'the horse was sired by Panorama out of a dam by Fair Trial. Would that be any good?'

'My dear boy,' said Eagally, 'you're getting the hang of it. It'd be just as good – though, as a matter of fact, there does happen to be one exception with that particular breeding. There is a horse of that breeding which has never won a race – but, as far as I know, only one. There must be the odd exception to every rule in racing – but they're so rare you can disregard them.'

'But how d'you know it's going to win this race? You'd have said the same for its fifth race, and it lost,' said Sally.

'Quite true,' said Eagally. 'I should have said the same, and I should have backed it and lost my money. But don't forget, it's run five races now. Past statistics show that, on an average, horses of a particular combination of breeding win their first race within their first three races. Accordingly, if they don't win in the first three races, the chances of win-ning the fourth are greatly increased, the fifth even more, and the sixth is as near to a certainty as doesn't matter – unless it's going to turn out to be an exception to the rule. Well, as I say, you're bound to get the odd exception, but you can pay for it out of your winnings on the others.'

'What's its name?' asked Roger. 'Not Capsule, by any chance?'

'No, it's called Fair View. There it is. Not much to look at, I agree. But if that horse doesn't win this race or the next, I'll eat my hat.'

'Is it in the next race as well, then? It'll be pretty tired, won't it?' asked Roger.

'No, I mean its next race. Anyway, I'm going to back it.'

'I was told that Capsule was going to win,' said Roger.

'Capsule?' said Eagally. 'I'll look it up. Let me see.' He referred to his little book. 'By Trimbush out of a Tiberius mare. Now, this is a good example of what I mean. That's a stayer. Perfect breeding for staying. Anything from one and a half miles upwards. But not for a sprint. Oh dear, no. Of course, it's only a two-year-old and they do win sometimes, but I wouldn't touch it.'

It was the general opinion of Roger's chambers that Eagally knew what he was talking about and they voted for Fair View and backed it. Then they went to the stands to watch the race.

'They're under starter's orders,' said the voice over the loudspeaker, and a moment later : 'They're off,' it said.

Fair View cannot have heard it. As soon as the tapes went up it turned round in the opposite direction.

'Hell,' said Eagally. 'w.r.s.t.n.p.'

'I beg your pardon?' said Sally.

'Tell you afterwards,' said Eagally.

The horses came towards them with more enthusiasm than they had shown in the paddock. About two hundred yards from the finish, one horse started to emerge from the others and it eventually won by a comfortable three lengths. It was Capsule.

'So sorry,' said Eagally, when the race was over. 'It's just one of those things. It would happen today. It was a certainty if it had only raced. I couldn't tell it was going to do that, could I?'

'You were going to tell me what you said when it happened,' said Sally. 'I thought it might be a private swear-word.'

'Oh, you mean "w.r.s.t.n.p." That simply means "whipped

round at start, took no part." I wish I knew when it was running again. It'd have to win. Couldn't lose, or my statistics are nonsense.'

'Have you ever considered that possibility?' asked Henry.

On the way down from the stands to the paddock, they met Mr Trent. He was talking to Mr Justice Kingsdown, whom he had waylaid, saying : 'Excuse me, Judge, aren't you Mr Justice Kingsdown?'

'Yes,' said the judge, who was a genial man. 'I must admit that. And who are you?'

'I don't suppose you would remember me, Judge,' Mr Trent had said. 'I was before you in chambers the other day – just as a pupil, you know. I didn't actually say anything. But I'd read all the papers. And I was quite sure you'd decide as you did.'

'How comforting,' said the judge. 'You don't happen to be quite sure who's going to win the next race, I suppose? Horses – I imagine – are less predictable than judges – though I have known a few decisions which could be classed as rank outsiders.'

At that moment Roger and his party were passing them.

'Hullo, Thursby,' said Mr Trent. 'The judge has just asked me for the winner of the next race. You can tell him I gave you the winner for the last. Hope you backed it.'

'Hullo, Thursby,' said the judge. 'And Blagrove. Quite a legal party. My daughter's somewhere about. I come to please her, you know. Doesn't mean very much to me.'

'The winner of the next race,' said Mr Trent, 'will in all probability be Cotton Wool – but it'll be a close thing between it and Madagascar. I shall back them both, if the odds are good enough.'

Eagally looked at his card. 'One and three-quarter miles,' he said. 'Now . . . the dam of Cotton Wool is by Gold Bridge – another great sire of sprinters. That won't do for one and three-quarter miles. It does occasionally happen with a very stout-hearted sire – Whiteway was an example – but normally if the dam's by Gold Bridge you can write off the horse as a stayer. Can't think why owners and trainers enter them for races of that distance. Now let's look at Madagascar. Sire of the dam was Sir Cosmo. That's almost as bad. No, I should write those off if I were you. Now, for a race of this description I'd choose something like – let me see –' and he consulted his little book.

'What about Roman Tour? By Tourbillon out of a Tiberius mare. Stay all the way from Land's End to John o' Groats. Let's see what it did last year.' He looked in another little book. 'Yes – not at all bad. Quite promising and, with that breeding, it'll stay for ever – that's the horse for my money.'

'Well,' said Roger, 'what's it to be?'

The prejudice against Mr Trent was so great that they voted for Eagally's choice. In due course they went to the stands to watch the race. Just before it started, Eagally said : 'There's only one thing I ought to have mentioned. There are only six horses in this race. That may mean that the race isn't truly run – isn't run at a fast enough pace. If that happens, it enables a horse which isn't a genuine stayer to win.'

'A horse like Madagascar, for instance,' said Roger, 'or Cotton Wool.'

'Could be,' said Eagally, 'but let's hope there's a smart gallop. I wonder who'll make the running.'

The race started and apparently no one wanted to make the running. The pace was rather like that of an underfed riding school going round Hyde Park. The crowd began to jeer and clap. But the funereal rate continued. It increased three or four furlongs from the end when two horses left the other four almost standing. They raced side by side for the last three hundred yards and made quite an exciting finish. There was no photo-finish apparatus, and the judge, after a moment's thought, awarded a dead heat – between Cotton Wool and Madagascar.

'What did I say?' said Mr Trent, as soon as he found Roger and Henry's party. 'Couldn't do much better than that.'

'Very good,' said Henry. 'Let's go to the paddock.' In the

paddock they found Mr Justice Kingsdown wandering round rather uncertainly – as though he couldn't find something he was looking for.

'Hullo, Judge.'

'Hullo.'

A pause.

'Er – I suppose,' said the judge, 'you haven't seen that rather extraordinary young man about anywhere? I was just wondering –'

'He was by the stands a minute ago, Judge,' said Roger.

'Thank you,' said the judge – and a moment or two later was seen to be moving towards the stands.

'I could have told him something for the next race,' said Eagally.

'Another certainty?' asked Henry.

'Well,' said Eagally, 'you can't blame me for the last two races. If a horse doesn't start, it can't win, can it? And in the last race you heard what the crowd thought of the pace. If there'd been fifteen runners it would have been a different story. Now, the next race is another sprint – six furlongs this time. Now, this is where statistics come in. Fair View didn't win.'

'No, we noticed that,' said Henry.

'This horse is of similar breeding – I don't suppose it means anything to you – but it's by Denturius out of a Panorama mare.'

'I assume it's never won,' said Roger.

'You're right,' said Eagally.

'But how many times has it tried?' said Henry.

'Now that's the point. Five times. Just like Fair View. Now it's statistically impossible for both horses to fail on the same day – let alone at the same meeting. It can't happen.'

'Suppose,' said Sally, 'it w.r.n.s. or whatever the correct expression was?'

'W.r.s.,' corrected Eagally. 'Statistically it can't.'

'But I suppose it can physically,' said Roger.

'Of course it can physically,' said Eagally. 'Physically it could die or break an artery or fall down or throw its jockey or charge the tapes and injure itself – or even win and be disqualified on an objection. But statistically it will win. It can't help it. That's what's so extraordinary.'

'Do the bookmakers know this?'

'Of course not. They only know which horses are backed most. That's all they care about. There it is, by the way. Better looking than Fair View, I should say. In pretty good condition.'

'D'you think you could tell it not to w.r.s. if I back it?' said Anne.

'I tell you,' said Eagally, 'that it can't whip round at the start or do anything else except win. You can't go wrong with statistics. Admittedly very occasionally there's an exception. But I can count them on one hand. Which reminds me. I had one last week. Now, you couldn't have two in a fortnight. It's absolutely impossible.'

'Do tell that to the horse,' said Henry.

'I don't blame you for laughing,' said Eagally, 'but, at the end of the race – you'll see. Most chaps are a bit cautious about giving their tips – take the newspapers. "If so-and-so can give the weight to such-and-such I think it should win. But I'm a little afraid of what's-his-name, and they say that t'other-'un is in the pink of condition." You must admit that I tell you quite definitely that the horse will win.'

'And I'm afraid,' said Henry, 'you must admit that so far it hasn't.'

'There have been special reasons,' said Eagally.

'I hope there isn't going to be one this time,' said Roger.

'It's statistically impossible,' said Eagally. 'It's a bit of luck, really. I've never known a case where the odds were so strongly in my favour. Let's hope it'll convince you.'

'I'm hoping to be convinced,' said Henry. 'And, to prove it, I shall put one pound to win on – what's its name?'

'Toothy Look,' said Eagally. 'Don't thank me now. Wait till it's won.'

'Very fair,' said Henry.

At that moment Donald arrived.

'Hullo,' he said and then, lowering his voice to a confidential whisper, he went on : 'My trainer says that Conference is bound to win if the boy can hold him in for the first mile.'

'What does that mean?' said Roger.

'Look,' said Donald, 'it's like this. By putting a boy on him he gets a seven-pound allowance – seven pounds less weight. Easier to run with less on your back, d'you follow?'

'Yes. That's very reasonable,' said Henry.

'Well, now, Conference is a little difficult for a boy to handle. He pulls like blazes, and if the boy can't hold him in he'll rush to the front and wear himself out. But if he can hold him in for a mile, he'll leave the others standing in the last two furlongs.'

'Well,' said Roger, 'what do we do about that?'

'I'll tell you. Some bookies will give you odds during the race. I'll put you near one or two who will. If Conference is in the rear at the end of a mile, put your shirt on him. But if he's right in front, leave him alone. He'll fold up in the last two furlongs and come in last. Got me?'

'Sounds plain sailing to me,' said Roger.

'Which race is it, the next one?' asked Henry.

'Now, Henry,' said Donald reprovingly, 'the next race is six furlongs. Eight furlongs make a mile. If he's to hold him in for a mile, stands to reason the race must be more than six furlongs.'

'Fair enough,' said Henry. 'Which race is it?'

'One after next,' said Donald. 'Now, don't forget. What are you doing for the next race? I saw old Kingsdown at the five-pound tote window.'

'He must have found Mr Trent,' said Roger.

'Come again,' said Donald.

'Mr Trent, in addition to knowing all the law worth knowing, knows all the winners worth knowing.'

'Who's Mr Trent?'

'He's the very learned pupil of my junior,' said Henry. 'He's worth meeting for a short time. I've no doubt he could give you a few hints.'

'Pity he's not your pupil, Roger,' said Donald. 'We'd teach him something.'

'My dear Donald,' said Roger, 'if Trent were my pupil I think I should retire from the Bar.' Then, in a slightly lower tone, he added : 'I'm doing that anyway, I suppose.'

'Don't come that one on me, Roger,' said Donald. 'See you later.'

Soon afterwards the chambers party and Eagally went to the stands to see the next race.

'They're under starter's orders,' was soon followed by 'They're off,' and this time Eagally's horse started with the rest.

'You see,' he said, 'no w.r.s. that time. It was statistically impossible. What did I tell you?'

'You said it would win,' said Henry.

'You'll see,' said Eagally. 'There it is – nicely tucked in on the rails – lying about sixth. Doesn't matter where it is. It's going to win.'

The horses charged on towards the winning post. A furlong out Toothy Look was still lying sixth.

'I wish it would hurry,' said Roger.

'Don't you worry,' said Eagally. 'He'll make his effort any moment. But it doesn't matter whether he does or he doesn't – he can't lose.'

'He seems to have a very reasonable chance of doing so at the moment,' said Henry.

A hundred yards from home Toothy Look's jockey made a very fine effort indeed. Unfortunately so did all the other jockeys, and Toothy Look duly passed the post – still sixth. But it's true to say that there was not more than a length between all six horses.

'First – number ten, second – number three, third – number eight,' said the voice over the loudspeaker.

'But Toothy Look was number ten,' said Sally.

'What did I tell you?' said Eagally.

'But I don't understand,' said Henry. Nor did the crowd. There were groans and howls of various kinds. The race had in fact been won by the favourite, but the judge had mistaken the favourite's colours for those of Toothy Look; they were very similar.

'Toothy Look didn't win that race,' said Roger.

'His number's in the frame,' said Eagally, 'and, as long as it's there, he won. Now, in any other race there'd be an objection of some kind, but there can't be in this one. It's statistically impossible. Just listen to the crowd. It's no good. The judge's decision is final.'

And it was. As they went from the stands to the totalisator to collect their winnings, they met an extremely angry judge, talking to Mr Trent, who seemed quite calm and collected. Mr Trent had correctly informed the judge which horse would come in first – but not which horse would win. The judge had lost five pounds.

'This is quite outrageous,' he said to Henry. 'There should be some method of appeal. I've always been told that racing was a crook's game. Now I know it.'

Five pounds is quite a lot of money to lose in that way.

'I couldn't agree with that, Judge, with respect,' said Mr Trent. 'There's nothing crooked about it, if I may say so. The judge made a mistake. That's all. It must happen sometimes. After all, judges are only human.'

'Our mistakes can be corrected,' snapped the judge. 'So should this judge's.'

'But, Judge,' said Mr Trent, 'surely there are occasions when a judge's decision is final and conclusive. Take, for instance –'

But the normally genial judge had had enough. Without another word he turned his back on Mr Trent and walked away.

'It's a shame,' said Mr Trent. 'Still, on his salary, it shouldn't hurt him all that much. I'm glad to say I didn't back it myself. I had a feeling about the race. How right I was. Any of you get the first home?'

'Well,' said Roger, 'we backed number ten – which was rather better.'

Not long afterwards, Donald came up to the party and, in a somewhat conspiratorial manner, invited them to follow him. He led them into Tattersalls' ring and pointed out a large and beery-faced-looking man who was already saying in substance – in a loud and ugly voice – that he would lay ten to one the field bar one. Donald also pointed out a much smaller man with a pointed face, sharp nose, and small moustache. He was saying – in a more staccato manner – that he also would be pleased to lay ten to one the field bar one.

'What does that mean?' said Anne.

'Don't you worry what it means,' said Donald. 'I'll tell you later. Now –' he said, in his most confidential evening voice to Roger and Henry, 'either of these two will give you a bet during the race. You'll hear them offering odds. All you've got to do when the field reaches that point – d'you see?' – and he pointed out on the course a place a little more than two furlongs from the winning post – 'all you've got to do is to say, "What'll you give on Conference?" But you'll have to be snappy, or you'll be too late. Come to think of it, you'd better do it a bit earlier. Say there –' and he pointed out a place about a hundred and fifty yards before the original one. 'Take whatever he offers, and put your silk gown on it,' he said to Henry. 'And you put your present one, Roger. You won't be needing it much longer. But, of course, only if Conference is in the rear. If he's in the lead, forget it and watch him come in last. Now – is everyone clear?'

Donald surveyed his employers and their ladies rather like a platoon sergeant giving instruction in musketry. Roger almost expected him to say 'any questions'. Satisfied that they knew what to do, Donald went hurriedly and erratically to see his trainer and the apprentice who was to ride Conference.

Roger and Anne, Henry and Sally, and Eagally, who had become one of the party, waited where they had been told.

'You haven't told us which one is statistically bound to win this race,' said Henry.

'Statistically,' said Eagally, with authority, 'any horse could win this race. That is why I haven't ventured to make any suggestions for it. That's one of the things I forgot to tell you. With my system, you can't back on every race. Oh, dear, no. You could certainly lose money that way.'

'And would it be very rude to inquire how much you've won this season so far?' asked Roger.

'Oh – I don't keep an exact account,' said Eagally. 'It isn't necessary. Statistically I know that I must have won and that's all that matters.'

'I should have thought it might have been worth having a check every now and then to see if the statistics had gone wrong,' said Henry.

'Statistics can't go wrong,' said Eagally. 'You've just seen a most interesting example of that.'

Not long afterwards, the horses went down to the post. Conference undoubtedly seemed to be anxious to get down to the start and indeed a good way past it. The boy on his back certainly was going to have his work cut out to hold him in.

'Hadn't we better check up with one of those bookies that they'll take a bet? Donald might have given us the wrong ones.' Roger went up to the red-faced man. 'Will you take a bet during the race?' he asked politely.

'What d'you think I'm something well here for?' said the bookie. 'Selling sweet peas, hokey-pokey penny a lump? Eights bar,' he yelled.

Roger retired.

'I don't think I cared for him much,' said Roger. 'I think I'll try the other one.'

The sharp-nosed man, in reply to Roger's question, said : 'Any particular horse?'

'Conference,' said Roger.

'I'll give you a hundred to six now,' said the bookie.

'I don't want to back it now,' said Roger.

'How much d'you want to put on?'

Roger thought for a moment. There were four of them. 'About a fiver, I suppose,' he said.

'Well, you can try,' said the bookie. 'But it all depends what's happening. If Conference runs the other way, I'll give you a hundred pounds to a sausage.'

Not at all confident that Donald's plan would work, Roger returned to the others. 'We'll have to be pretty quick off the mark,' he said, 'or the race will be over before we've understood what they've said.'

A minute later the white flag was up, and then they were off.

'Oh, dear,' said Anne. And well she might. For the impatient Conference had virtually seized the reins out of the little boy's hands and was tearing for home as fast as he could go. He sprang into a two lengths' lead almost at once. This he increased to three, four, and, finally, to ten lengths – and by the time the vital point was reached he was still that much up.

'Tens bar,' shouted the red-faced bookie.

But the chambers party did not move. Round the bend came Conference with its little passenger – who had long ceased to try to hold him – looking rather like a little apple with a coloured cap.

'What a shame,' said Sally. 'It looks to me as though he's going to win all the same.'

By this time the jockeys on the other horses were doing everything they could to encourage their mounts to catch up Conference. They certainly made up some ground, but not enough, and, in due course, as though he knew where he was going, Conference safely delivered his little apple to the winner's enclosure. Donald was there to greet him – in a state of great excitement. His trainer was equally pleased.

'Sorry I couldn't hold him in,' said the little apple.

'If you win a race you're meant to win,' said the trainer, 'you don't have to apologize.'

The chambers party came to offer Donald their congratulations.

'How much did you put on?' he asked.

They stared at him for a moment. Then Roger said: 'Nothing, of course. You told us.'

'Sir, sir, sir,' said Donald. 'But I didn't tell you not to use your loaf, did I? It was obvious he was going to win.'

'You told me,' said Henry, 'that if he were leading at the spot you pointed out, we were not to touch him.'

'Sir,' said Donald, in what appeared to him to be a dignified manner, 'the trouble is you boys don't understand racing.'

'I think we can agree to that,' said Roger.

But it had been a good day, all the same, and he had found plenty of opportunity in between the races to be with Anne alone.

Donald, too, had had an exhilarating day. He had never won a race before. His wife put him to bed.

Chapter 17

A QUESTION OF CONFIDENCE

THE next week was a particularly busy one for Roger. He was in court every day, had a large number of conferences, and had an infinite amount of paper work to do. But it all sat very lightly on him now. Towards the end of the week Mr Glacier and Mr Plumb came to see him to report progress.

'If you ask me,' said Mr Glacier, 'what you call a little bird must have spoken to the inspector.'

'The trap didn't come off?'

'I will tell you exactly what happened,' said Mr Glacier, 'and,' he added, 'you can be sure I am speaking the truth as everything which was said was recorded by tape machine.'

'Well, what happened?' said Roger.

'I duly attended the interview,' said Mr Glacier, 'and this is what happened. The inspector began :

' "This is all very irregular. What is it you want to see me about?"

'I said : "I hoped we might be able to come to an understanding."

' "About what?" he said.

' "You know what about, inspector," I said.

' "I certainly don't," he said, "and I must warn you that anything you say now may be given in evidence at your trial."

'Well, Mr Thursby, as you may have observed, I am not usually at a loss for words, but I was beginning to find myself – how do you say? – against a blank wall. It appeared obvious to me that any attempt to bribe him at that moment would have been quite hopeless. He was obviously on his guard. So I decided to play one more card – to see if at any rate I could take one trick. "I don't mind what you give in evidence, inspector," I said, "so long as it is the truth. Why did you not tell the truth about the money I gave you?" He did not answer for a moment. Then : "What do you mean?" he said. "You know quite well what I mean, inspector," I said. "You know I gave you thirty pounds and thirty-five pounds, not twenty pounds and twenty-five pounds. And perhaps you would be interested to know that the whole of our conversation is now being listened to by your superintendent." ' Mr Glacier paused.

'Good Lord ! What did he say?'

'Nothing,' said Mr Glacier. 'Not only words failed him, but blood, or whatever it is, also failed him. He fainted. Fortunately he fell to the ground with a crash. I might perhaps have saved him, but I thought that we should then miss the noise of his fall in the microphone. So I let – how do you say? – nature take its course. He was not much hurt. But, of course, gravity will have its way and the inspector is a tall man.'

'What happened then?' asked Roger.

'Everything seemed to happen at once. The superintendent and Chief Constable who had been listening to the conversation rushed in to assist the inspector. At first they took no notice of me. But when they had revived the inspector and had put some plaster on the cut on his head, they appeared to notice me.

' "Can I be of any further assistance?" I asked most politely.

' "Kindly leave this station at once, sir, and don't come back," said the Chief Constable.

' "But really," I protested, "what have I done? Is it my fault if the inspector faints?"

' "You have been guilty of a disgraceful breach of confidence in telling the inspector that the conversation was being overheard."

' "You were never going to tell him then?" I asked.

' "Leave the station, sir," said the Chief Constable.

'So, of course, I left and at once reported to Mr Plumb and he has brought me to you as soon as possible.'

'I have spoken to the Director's office,' said Mr Plumb, who had some justification for the mournful way in which he said it, 'and I'm afraid they don't like us at all, not at all.'

'Dear, dear,' said Roger. 'All is finished between us, I suppose, and the prosecution is going on as hard as ever. The armistice is over, the gloves are off, the detectives have gone back to Scotland Yard, and the fight is on.'

'You sound remarkably cheerful,' said Mr Glacier. 'I hope with reason. You will permit me to remind you once again that it is my wife and I who rot in gaol, not you.'

'Well,' said Roger who, for reasons wholly unconnected with Mr Glacier, was continuously cheerful, 'we shall do our best to prevent that happening. And I'm bound to say that, short of having the prosecution called off, we haven't done so badly.'

'You are satisfied then?' said Mr Plumb. 'I must say I never thought you would be happy about the present position.'

'Happier than either of you appear to be,' said Roger.

'Let me remind you yet again – at the risk of repetition,' began Mr Glacier, 'that it is –'

'No, I won't,' said Roger. 'I remember perfectly. It's you who'll go to gaol if you're convicted. Quite right. So it will be. As to that, all I can say is that I think you've a very good chance of not going to gaol, but, if you do, it's entirely your own fault for giving money to policemen.'

'Our little Melanie,' began Mr Glacier.

'Whether it was your little Melanie or not – and I doubt whether anyone will really believe that little Melanie came into the story at all – but, even if she did, you must have known perfectly well that to give sixty-five pounds to police officers is a wrong thing to do. None the less, I think you've a very good chance of getting away with it.'

'You think we will be acquitted?'

'I think it very possible. Nothing, of course, is certain, but the case has got to be proved and, apart from your word and your wife's, we have three things in our favour – and there might have been a fourth. First, there's your police constable; secondly, there's the fact that we went to the police straight away and that they set a trap for their own people; thirdly, the inspector fainted. It's quite true that the sudden knowledge that his superiors sufficiently mistrusted him to make them set a trap for him might have been such a shock to him that he lost consciousness for a moment, but, of course, it's also possible that your statement about the money, coupled with the knowledge that he was being listened to, had that effect. He, of course, will give the former explanation, but when you add the police constable's evidence to it, it'll shake the jury pretty considerably, I should say.'

'What is the fourth point that you might have had?'

'Mr Plumb,' said Roger, 'did you tell Mr Glacier about your conversation with the Chief Constable? The one you consulted me about?'

'Yes, I did, as a matter of fact,' said Mr Plumb. 'Before I told you about it. Shouldn't I have?'

'Am I to understand,' said Mr Glacier, 'that my lawyers have some doubt whether they should tell me something they have learned in the conduct of proceedings on my behalf?'

'It was said to Mr Plumb in confidence,' said Roger.

'Confidence,' said Mr Glacier. 'And when did I give you – how do you say? – authority to keep things secret from me?'

'Mr Plumb acted as many other solicitors would have acted. The Chief Constable said something to him and then added that it was in confidence and Mr Plumb agreed. Litigation could not be conducted if lawyers could not trust each other and say things in confidence to one another.'

'First,' said Mr Glacier, 'the Chief Constable is not a lawyer.'

'The principle is the same in this case,' said Roger.

'Very well,' said Mr Glacier, 'I will assume that it is. Is not litigation, as you call it, proceedings between two persons over some civil dispute? Is a prosecution where one side may go to gaol or, indeed, be hanged, litigation?'

'You may be right, Mr Glacier, that litigation strictly

means civil proceedings. But criminal lawyers must be able to trust one another just the same.'

'I do not care two figs whether they trust one another or not. I do not mind what are the – I think you call them – the ethics of the legal profession. I who stand in danger of being sent to prison demand – yes, demand, I say – that all facts which are in my favour shall be used to help to secure my acquittal. Now I am right in thinking, am I not, that this fourth matter to which you referred is the statement to Mr Plumb that in effect the inspector was already a suspected person? I am right, am I not?' he repeated.

'Yes,' said Roger, 'you're quite right.'

'And am I further right in thinking that, in your view, if that further fact were brought to the attention of the jury, it would raise even more our chances of being acquitted?'

'That is quite true,' said Roger.

'Then,' said Mr Glacier, 'I demand that it be used.'

'Demand is a strong word, Mr Glacier,' said Roger.

'The occasion requires the use of strong words.'

'I told you,' said Roger, 'that I reserved the right to throw up the case if it was not conducted in a proper manner.'

'You, of course, have that right,' said Mr Glacier, 'and let me make it plain that I should be very sorry indeed if you did – how did you say? – throw it up. Indeed, I demand that unless I have done something wrong or require you to do something wrong, that you do not do so.'

'I wish you wouldn't keep on using that word "demand",' said Roger. 'I want to help you as far as I properly can, but whenever you say "demand" I feel like pushing you out of the room. You will please assume that I will do everything that is right and proper to secure your acquittal.'

'Do you not consider it right and proper that a fact which could affect the jury's verdict should be put before them? How can you have these so-called confidences in matters where a man's liberty – or, indeed, his life – the principle is the same – is at stake?'

'It is not an easy matter,' said Roger.

'I see no difficulty about it at all,' said Mr Glacier. 'Let us suppose, for example, that you have a client charged with a crime and the counsel for the prosecution told you – in confidence – in absolute confidence – that, as a matter of fact, the prosecution knew that your client was not guilty but that, as they could not prove the case against the guilty man and the public wanted a – what is the word? – a scapegoat, they were going to try to secure a conviction against your client – supposing the charge were murder – the penalty death – suppose your client were convicted and hanged – would you think you had acted properly in keeping your learned friend's confidence or not?'

'Such a thing could never happen in this country,' said Roger.

'But suppose it did – strange things do occur – would you keep the matter told you in confidence?'

Roger did not answer at once.

'No doubt you would seek to be relieved of the obligation to keep the matter in confidence, you would see your opponent and endeavour to obtain a release from him and you would have sound arguments to urge him, but supposing all your efforts were in vain, what then? Would you keep his confidence – with a man's life at stake?'

'No,' said Roger, 'in a strong case like that I don't think I could. But that isn't this case. It is not a case of life or death and the statement made is nothing like so outrageous or unworthy of confidence as the one in the case you've suggested.'

'One thing at a time,' said Mr Glacier. 'You say it is not a case of life or death. But is there any difference in what you lawyers are pleased to call principle between loss of liberty and loss of life? Who are you to say what the consequences of loss of liberty may be to me or my wife? Prison may have a – what is the word? – a permanent effect on some people, it may kill others. This is not a criticism of your prisons. I refer to loss of liberty. So first I say, how do you distinguish betwen death and imprisonment?'

'There is obviously a difference in fact,' said Roger, 'but in principle you may be right.'

'Very well then. Now, as to the nature of the statement. You pride yourselves in this country on the prosecution being fair. Is it fair, do you think, to call as the main witness for the prosecution a man whom you suspect of dishonesty, to put him before the jury as a man of upright character and not to tell the defence of your suspicions? Is that fair? And, if it is not, is the statement made by the Chief Constable any more worthy of confidence than the one that I suggested?'

'Mr Glacier,' said Roger, 'I'm bound to say you put your point of view very ably. I shall have to think this one out. It's not at all an easy decision to have to make.'

'I am quite sure,' said Mr Glacier, 'that you will consider the matter most carefully before coming to a decision. Should your decision be adverse to my interests, is it possible for me to consult your society or institute on the matter?'

'The Bar Council, you mean?' said Roger. 'There would not be time to get a ruling of the Bar Council before the case is heard. But I would certainly speak to the Chairman about it, if you wished. Indeed, I may do so in any event. I entirely see your point of view, but the legal profession could not be carried on without rules and the rules must be kept.'

'Even if the result is that innocent persons are hanged or sent to prison? Permit me to say,' said Mr Glacier, 'that an amendment of any such rules in a civilized community would seem to be highly desirable. But, of course, no such amendment could be made before the trial . . . you will say. You will, no doubt, send me a copy to the particular prison where I am rotting.'

'I don't know why you're so convinced that you'll be convicted if we don't use the statement. I should have thought that your clear conscience would have made you more optimistic.'

'Who said I had a clear conscience?' asked Mr Glacier. 'You have already pointed out to me that it was wrong to give money to policemen.'

Eventually it was arranged that Roger should consider

what course he was proposing to adopt and that he would let Mr Plumb know when he had made up his mind.

As soon as he could, Roger went in to see Henry.

'I gather we're enemies, again,' said Henry.

'So do I,' said Roger. 'But there's an awkward thing I want to talk to you about. D'you think you could get Digby over? It's rather serious.'

'O.K.,' said Henry. 'Are you sure you wouldn't like his able assistant Mr Trent as well?'

'I think we'll be able to manage without him some-how,' said Roger. 'We can always send for him if we get stuck.'

So a meeting took place the next day between Henry and his junior Digby, and Roger.

'So sorry I couldn't get down last time,' said Digby, 'but I feel sure I was most ably represented.'

'Incredibly so,' said Henry.

'I shouldn't have liked you to miss Tony Trent,' said Digby. 'He has to be heard to be believed. I confess he fascinates me. If I had the time I could listen to him for hours. Well, what's the trouble? Your Mr Glacier, if I may say so, is a pretty good stinker.'

'And a very able one,' said Henry.

'He's certainly that,' said Roger, 'whatever else he may be . . . as to which I don't feel called on to make any ad-missions.'

'The Chief Constable's hopping mad,' said Henry.

'I don't altogether blame him,' said Digby.

'I think you're being a bit unfair,' said Roger. 'No one had told him not to give the game away to the inspector. The Chief Constable wouldn't have minded if the inspector had been caught. What he, of course, is livid about is not catch-ing the inspector and letting the inspector know that they'd tried to catch him. Must make it sort of awkward for him, I agree. But that isn't altogether my man's fault.'

'Yes – but look at the way he did it,' said Henry.

'Did what?' asked Roger.

'Look,' said Henry, 'if you ask me, old Glacier knew the

game was up and that if he just asked the inspector why he said he'd received forty-five pounds when, in fact, he'd had sixty-five pounds the inspector would simply have denied it. So what does he do? He puts the question to him and, before he has time to answer, he fires at him point-blank about the Chief Constable and superintendent listening in. Well – he couldn't have known it'd be such a success and that the inspector would faint, but he must have hoped that by following up the one question with the other he'd be bound to shake the inspector, and no doubt he hoped that he'd yammer for a bit. And even for the most upright inspector in the world it must be a pretty considerable shock to be told suddenly that a criminal is being used as a bait and that the conversation's being tapped. He'd no other cards to play, so he brought out that one.'

'Well,' said Roger, 'we shall see, my dear fellow, we shall see. No doubt you will ask Mr Glacier the question when he gives evidence. I promise you I won't tell him what to answer.'

'No need,' said Henry. 'He's quite capable of taking care of himself. I must say I don't blame the old Chief Constable. To blow the gaff like that was a bit steep.'

Roger suddenly had a horrible thought. 'I hope he doesn't think it was anything to do with me,' he said.

'Well,' said Henry, 'I must confess I don't think he likes you very much.'

'Blast and curse,' said Roger. I must see Anne and explain, he thought. Confound Glacier, confound everything. Why must Anne be mixed up in it? I hope she'll believe me. Oh – good Lord! – 'Where's the catch, Mr Thursby? Do you tell me now or later or do I have to find it out for myself?' 'There's no catch, Chief Constable.' 'Bait with no hook, eh? You're not a fisherman, I imagine.' Bait with no hook! Here was the hook with a vengeance. He'll never believe that I wasn't behind it all. Anne will believe me – I hope – but her father will think me a scoundrel. She might marry me just the same ... but it would be horrible for her – she's fond of her father. Blast Mr Glacier – though, to be fair, I'd never have met Anne but for him. Oh, well – I shall have to do something about it.

'I hope you told him it wasn't anything to do with me,' said Roger.

'I haven't seen him yet,' said Henry. 'I got it from the Director.'

'Well – do tell him when you get the chance,' said Roger. 'It's rather important to me, as a matter of fact.'

'O.K.,' said Henry. 'I see. I'll do my best.'

'Is that all you wanted me for,' said Digby, 'as I've got to go to Brixton to see a friend?'

'No,' said Roger, 'that last bit made me forget what I really wanted to see you about. But that makes it worse than ever. I really don't know what to do. Look, this is the trouble.' He then told Henry and Digby what the problem was, putting all the arguments for and against the evidence being used.

'Of course,' he said, 'the Chief Constable shouldn't have said afterwards that it was in confidence. He ought to have said "I'll tell you this in confidence but not otherwise." That might have been different. But, however he did it, old Plumb said he would treat it in confidence. And if you say you're going to treat a thing in confidence, you've got to keep your word. It isn't like a contract. You don't have to have consideration for it. Moreover, if Plumb had said "You should have said that before, you didn't say it was in confidence and I'm going to use it," the Chief Constable would probably have cried off the whole thing. So by keeping silent Plumb in effect assured the Chief Constable that the statement would be kept in confidence. Then, like a blithering idiot, he goes and tells the client. That was a breach of confidence to begin with, but he didn't realize it. But let's assume he didn't tell the client. Let's assume only Plumb and I knew it, and we'd agreed to treat it in confidence – have we the right to do so if a man may be hanged or go to gaol if we do? I'm bound to say I think Glacier's right in saying there's no distinction in principle between death and prison. My natural instinct, of course, tells me that I can't use the statement – but then, as Glacier would say, it's easy for me. I don't have to rot in gaol. What do you each think about it?'

'I don't see any difficulty,' said Digby. 'It was said in confidence and that's an end of it.'

'What do you think, Henry?'

'I don't think it's as simple as that,' said Henry. 'As Roger says, it's easy enough for us. We stick to our rules and say what fine fellows we are, puff our chests out and say you can always trust a member of the Bar – good old Thursby – he'll never let you down; meantime, Mr Thursby's client is duly executed or sent to prison for life. I certainly wouldn't puff my chest out after that.'

'Confidence means confidence,' said Digby. 'If you can't trust a member of the Bar, you might as well shut up shop. That's where it's different from business. You can rely on a reputable member of the Bar not to do a dirty trick. If you couldn't, it'd be hopeless. I don't know what you're worried about. It was said in confidence, and that's an end of it. That's what I think, anyway; I'm not a lawyer like you chaps, but I know the answer to that one.'

'If the charge were murder and you were in my shoes, would you refuse to use the statement?' asked Roger.

'Of course I would,' said Digby. 'Shouldn't even think of using it. Fight hard but fight clean, I say.'

'And you wouldn't worry if you hadn't used the statement and your client were hanged?'

'Not in the least,' said Digby. 'He'd have been guilty ten times over anyway if he were convicted. People make too much fuss about these things, I think. They hardly ever get to the dock if they're innocent and, if there's a chance in a million that they're innocent, they get off. Even if I happen to be defending them. No – give them a fair trial, I say, but no more. They're ninety-nine per cent guilty, but I quite agree they should have a proper trial and, if there's any loophole, by all means let them get away with it. But don't lean over backwards to push the guilty ones out of the dock.'

'Well,' said Roger, 'what d'you say to *this* point of

Glacier's? You say they should have a fair trial. If you have a witness who's got a previous conviction you'd tell counsel for the defence, wouldn't you?'

'Of course.'

'Well – what's the difference in principle? You've got a witness whom you distrust. The defence can't know that. So, unless you tell them, the witness is put forward as a person of integrity.'

'If you haven't got anything against him, he *is* a person of integrity. Suspicion isn't enough. The Chief Constable suspected the inspector. All right. But he may have been wrong. He'd no evidence. If you had to tell the defence of every witness you weren't too happy about, where would it stop? There's a limit, you know.'

'Has he convinced you, Henry?' asked Roger.

'I can't say he has,' said Henry. 'I'm glad I'm not in your shoes. I'm hanged if I'd know what I'd do. I'm bound to say that I'm inclined to think that, when the acid test is applied, there can't be such a thing as confidence in criminal matters any more than there can be "without prejudice" conversations or letters. I suppose the answer is that, if anything is said in confidence in a criminal matter, the confidence must be kept if it's possible. But, in the last resort, the man in the dock comes first.'

'I can only say,' said Digby, 'that with the greatest respect and all that I profoundly disagree. To my mind the seal of confidence is binding for ever and in all instances and there are no exceptions.'

'Well, there you are, Roger,' said Henry, 'the Court's divided. On the whole and without a great deal of confidence – no pun intended – I agree with you, Roger, that, if you think it absolutely essential in the interests of your client to use the statement, you must use it.'

'I can only repeat – with considerable confidence,' said Digby, 'that such a point of view, if adopted generally, would be disastrous for the legal profession.'

'There I don't agree,' said Roger, 'because this kind of thing will only happen very, very occasionally. It's never happened to you, I suspect, and you're at the Criminal Bar. It's certainly never happened to me before, and I'll be very surprised if it happens again. Well – I'm most grateful to you both. I really have to make up my own mind.'

'I'll be very rude to you,' said Digby, 'if you don't make it up the right way.'

'I don't care two hoots about that,' thought Roger . . . 'but Anne's father – oh, Lord . . . Anne's father.'

Chapter 18

THE MISSING WITNESS

ROGER'S other work fortunately prevented him from thinking too much of his pressing personal and professional problems. Among his minor activities in Court was an appearance in the Divorce Court to do an undefended divorce case of some difficulty. It was before a new County Court judge and, as Roger's case was fairly high in the list, he went there early to see how quickly that particular judge got through his list. He was an unknown quantity. Some judges can quite comfortably dispose of twenty or thirty undefended divorce cases in one day. Others have their work cut out to deal with a dozen. It rather depends on the approach. The approach of Judge Renfrew was not known. Roger found that Crabtree was in the first case and he arrived in time to hear him saying :

'Oh – my Lord – I'm afraid I shall be in some difficulty in this case – as an essential witness, who has been subpoenaed – I can prove it, my Lord – is apparently not here, and I'm not sure how much I can prove without him . . . in due course I shall ask your Lordship to take steps against the witness but, in the meantime, my Lord, I was wondering – I was wondering –' He paused for so long that Judge Renfrew said :

'You were wondering, Mr Crabtree?'

'Yes – my Lord – I was wondering –'

'Quite, Mr Crabtree – but what?'

'I was wondering, my Lord – I was wondering –'

'So am I now, Mr Crabtree.'

'That's very good of your Lordship.'

'Not at all, Mr Crabtree. Were you perhaps wondering if I would hear such evidence as you have, and see how far it gets us?'

'That was it exactly,' said Mr Crabtree. 'It is very good of your Lordship.'

'Not at all, Mr Crabtree. At any rate it's stopped us both wondering. Call your evidence and we'll see how far you can take it.'

Crabtree proceeded to call his evidence and, apart from proving that his client had duly married the respondent, that they had lived at various places and had no children, and that the photograph produced was a photograph of the respondent, and the signature produced was his signature – he proved practically nothing.

'And now, my Lord,' said Crabtree, 'I propose to prove that the missing witness was duly served with the subpoena and then I shall ask your Lordship to take steps.'

'Very well, Mr Crabtree.'

The process server was duly called and he duly proved that the witness had been served with the subpoena and provided with conduct money.

'And now, my Lord,' said Crabtree, 'I ask your Lordship to take steps.'

'Yes, Mr Crabtree, what steps?' asked the judge.

'Oh, my Lord,' said Crabtree, waving his arm as if to express something, 'oh, my Lord –' he repeated – 'steps – against the witness.'

'Yes, Mr Crabtree – what steps?'

'Oh, my Lord,' said Crabtree, waving his arm again – 'there must be steps.'

'No doubt,' said the judge, 'but what?'

'Oh, my Lord,' said Crabtree, and waited for inspiration. After it had failed to come for the space of about ten seconds, the judge said :

'Would you like a few minutes to consider the matter and I'll take another case in the meantime?'

'That is most kind of your Lordship. It would be most helpful.'

'Call the next case then, please,' said the judge, 'and let me know when you are ready, Mr Crabtree.'

'Thank you, my Lord,' said Crabtree, and went hurriedly to the Bar Library.

While Roger was waiting, Donald came up to him. 'You're all right in QB4 for the moment and you're quite safe in the Court of Appeal till this afternoon. You'd better wait here and I'll watch the non-jury.'

'Thanks,' said Roger.

Judge Renfrew had disposed of three more cases when Crabtree returned and informed his Lordship that he was now ready.

'Yes, Mr Crabtree?' said the judge.

'My Lord, if your Lordship will be good enough to look at Rayden at page 347, you will see that your Lordship can issue a warrant for the arrest of the witness.'

The judge referred to the passage. 'Yes, Mr Crabtree, I see the statement. Can you tell me under what rule of Court or statute the power arises?'

'Oh, my Lord,' began Crabtree, 'oh, my Lord –'

'Yes?' said the judge.

'Oh, my Lord,' Crabtree repeated, 'I'm sure it wouldn't appear in Rayden if it weren't right.'

'So am I,' said the judge. 'It is in the highest degree improbable. But I must know the rule or the statute or whatever it is before I interfere with the liberty of the subject.'

'But, my Lord, it says quite definitely here –' said Crabtree.

'I know, I know,' said the judge, 'but it gives no authority for the proposition and, although I don't doubt it in the least, I must know what it is.'

'Well, my Lord –'

'Yes, Mr Crabtree?'

'Well, my Lord –'

'Mr Crabtree, would you like me to put the case back again for you to find out the authority?'

'That would be most kind of your Lordship.'

'Very well, Mr Crabtree. Let me know when you are ready.'

The judge continued with another case and several further cases, including Roger's. As he finished Roger's case, Crabtree returned and, as he had not yet been summoned by Donald, Roger waited to see what would happen.

'My Lord,' said Crabtree, 'I've made an exhaustive search and I'm afraid I can't actually find the authority your Lordship wants, but I'm quite sure the learned editor of Rayden would not have put it in unless —'

'So am I, Mr Crabtree, but, as I said before, I must be satisfied before I have people arrested. I see that the subpoena itself says nothing about arrest but only about forfeiting one hundred pounds.'

'Yes, my Lord.'

'Well, what d'you want me to do?'

'Well, of course, my Lord,' said Crabtree, 'if this came under the Rules of the Supreme Court, it would be quite easy to show your Lordship —'

'But it does come under the Rules of the Supreme Court, Mr Crabtree, subject to any modification by statute or the rules of this Division of the Supreme Court.'

'Oh, well, in that case, my Lord, I ask your Lordship to take steps —'

'But under what Rule of the Supreme Court, Mr Crabtree?'

'I'm afraid, my Lord, I haven't the actual rule in front of me — perhaps your Lordship wouldn't mind —'

'Certainly, Mr Crabtree, I'll take another case.'

The judge took several more cases and eventually Crabtree returned, looking rather dejected.

'I'm afraid, my Lord,' he said, 'that with such little time at my disposal I haven't been able to find —'

'Well, Mr Crabtree, wouldn't it be best if I adjourned this case for fourteen days for you to go into the matter? I should make it plain that I feel quite sure you are right in saying that, if a man deliberately disobeys a subpoena, he can be dealt with in an appropriate manner. Justice could not be administered if there weren't procedure to compel witnesses to give evidence. But I'm sure you'll understand that I must see the power under which I am acting before I deprive people of their liberty.'

'Of course, my Lord,' said Crabtree. 'It is very good of your Lordship, and I will gratefully accept your Lordship's suggestion of a fourteen-day adjournment.'

'Very well,' said the judge. 'Adjourned for fourteen days.'

Just as the judge was about to start another case, and Crabtree was about to leave the Court, a man, who had been there all the time, suddenly addressed the judge from a seat in the middle of the Court.

'May I speak?' he asked. 'I didn't like to interrupt before, but was it me you were talking about?'

It was the witness.

Chapter 19

COLONEL MADDERLEY'S OPINION

—

THE Chief Constable of Carpshire was talking to Anne. 'I'm sorry, Anne,' he said. 'I know how you must feel. If you're fond of him, there's nothing I can do, or would do for that matter, to stop you marrying him. And it won't alter you and me – I hope not – not as far as I'm concerned. But I can't have him in the house. I know I'm not a clever chap like he is – thank God I'm not – but I have a code. I dare say he laughs at soldiers and policemen. Blithering lot of idiots he thinks them. A lot of Blimps. All right, perhaps they are . . . and I'm one of them. But there are just certain things a chap doesn't do. And once anyone lets me down I'm finished with him. I'm not a fellow who wants revenge – I don't want my own back or anything of that sort – I just have nothing more to do with him. And that's all there is to it. I don't even say I'm in the right. If you like, he's in the right and I'm in the wrong. Be that as it may . . . when a chap does what he's done, I'm finished and that's all there is to it. I'm sorry, Anne, I really am. But that's the way it is and I'm too old to change now.'

'I understand, father,' said Anne. 'But why d'you blame Roger for it all? I'm sure he wouldn't do anything that was disgraceful or underhand for himself or anyone else. I don't know him well, but I'm sure he's not like that.'

'You don't know him well, Anne. You say so yourself. How can you tell? I judge by what a man does. It's the only way I know. Not the way he looks or what he says – but what he does. Simple, if you like, but it's the only way of judging a man that I've found any good. Your Roger could, I've no doubt, talk me into a cocked hat. He could play old Harry with me in the witness box – or in ordinary conversation if you like. I don't pretend to be any good at talking and he is – and if you ask me . . . I'm sorry to say this – he's a damned sight too good at it.'

'Father,' said Anne, 'please.'

'It's no good, Anne, and it's much better to face the facts. You and I always have. He sat in that chair you're in now. "Where's the catch?" I said. "There isn't one," he said. And then, when we'd had our chat, he said : "D'you still think there's a catch?" I trusted him, Anne, and his solicitor. The whole thing, if you ask me, was a thundering fraud. Clever, mind you – darned clever. It would take a clever chap to work that one out.'

'If I could show you it wasn't Roger's fault, father, you would change, wouldn't you ?'

'My dear, dear Anne, of course I would. D'you think I like this between us – well, it isn't between us, because nothing could be – but interfering with us, hurting us both; of course I don't. But it's facts, Anne, facts. If you can show me facts are not facts, black is white and white is black – if you show it me, not by words or fine speeches but by things I can see and know – nobody will be better pleased than I shall be. But you can't do it, Anne. Facts can't lie. People can.'

Later that day Anne spoke to Roger.

'I'm sure if you came to see him, you'd make him understand,' she said.

'I can't during the case, Anne,' he said. 'He wouldn't see me anyway – and he'd be quite right at the moment. But, as soon as it's over, of course I will.'

And with that they both had to be satisfied.

Chapter 20

THE GLACIERS ON TRIAL

———

THE case of the Glaciers went on again the next week, but in a very different atmosphere. No cooperation this time between prosecution and defence, and no race meeting afterwards. Eventually the prosecution completed its case. Roger elected to call no evidence and both Mr and Mrs Glacier were committed for trial at the next Carpshire Assizes. They were both granted bail. Before the day of the trial they had a final conference with Roger.

'Well, Mr Thursby,' said Mr Glacier, 'have you made up your mind about this statement?'

'Yes,' said Roger. 'I have come to the conclusion that, if you require me to use it, it is my duty to do so – however much I may personally dislike doing it.'

'That simplifies matters,' said Mr Glacier. 'I require you to use it. I am extremely sorry for any inconvenience or embarrassment in which it may involve you. It is – how would you say? – just one of those things. And now, may I ask you yet again – what do you consider our chances are of being acquitted?'

'I think they're good,' said Roger. 'But naturally there's no certainty about it.'

'Ah, well,' said Mr Glacier, 'certainty is more than I could ask for, but I confess I should prefer to have certainty one way or the other.'

'You would prefer to have certainty that you would be convicted,' said Mr Plumb, in some amazement, 'than a reasonable chance that you will be acquitted?'

'We are on bail,' said Mr Glacier. 'The world is a large place. Now, please don't agitate yourself, Mr Plumb,' he added hastily, when he saw Mr Plumb's hand and handkerchief starting up. 'I have no intention of – how do you call it? – jumping my bail.'

'It wouldn't be much use if you did,' said Roger. 'You'd only be picked up some time and extradited.'

'Do extradition treaties extend then to all countries and for all offences?' asked Mr Glacier. 'It is only what you would call an academic question,' he added.

'I don't know,' said Roger. 'I haven't looked it up.'

'As a matter of fact,' said Mr Glacier, 'I have made some research into the subject. I have surrendered my passport, but not my British Museum library ticket. It is, I find, a good thing to consider every aspect of a case. But pray do not be alarmed, Mr Plumb. I have the utmost confidence in Mr Thursby and, of course, in your good self, and, that being so, my visits to the British Museum can be considered of no practical significance. Though, of course, I am one who thinks that knowledge is never wasted.'

The case came on for trial very shortly after the conclusion of the proceedings before the magistrates. Mr Justice Kingsdown was the judge. There were two charges against each defendant. They pleaded Not Guilty, were given the usual permission to sit down, and the trial began. Henry, having informed the judge and jury that he appeared for the prosecution with his learned friend Mr Gerald Digby, and that the defendants had the advantage of being represented by his learned friend Mr Thursby, went on to tell them the facts, as alleged by the prosecution. He made no reference to the trap which had been set for the inspector and simply outlined the case as it had been before Roger and Mr Plumb went to see the Chief Constable. Before calling the evidence in support of his opening speech, Henry said this :

'Members of the jury, we pride ourselves in this country that corruption is rare and that, where we find it, we do all in our power to stamp it out. It is one of the most insidious of all evils, it is difficult to detect and, once it starts, no one knows how far it will go. No people are more likely to be tempted by corruption than the police force and it is vital that we should have a police force which is resistant to all such attempts. I venture to suggest to you, members of the jury, that – when you have heard the evidence in this case – you will come to the conclusion that it is a classic case of attempted corruption . . . by a rich man anxious to escape from the consequences of a breach of the licensing laws. Mr and Mrs Glacier no doubt find that money can buy them many things that poorer people cannot have and, in due course, I shall ask you to say that they tried to buy something which in this country is not for sale.'

Henry then called the inspector to give evidence. In examination-in-chief he said very much what he said in the Magistrate's Court. Then Henry sat down and he was cross-examined by Roger.

'How is your head?' was Roger's first question.

The judge and the jury looked surprised at the question, which, of course, was Roger's intention.

'It's better thank you,' said the inspector.

'A nasty bump, I'm afraid,' said Roger.

'Not too bad,' said the inspector.

'I take it,' said the judge, 'the jury and I are going to be let into the secret some time.'

'Of course, my Lord,' said Roger. 'You hit your head against a desk and cut it, I'm afraid?' he went on.

'Yes,' said the inspector.

'That was about three weeks ago, was it not?'

'Yes.'

'You were having an interview with the defendant, Mr Glacier, were you not?'

'Yes, I was.'

'The man who is supposed to have tried to bribe you?'

'Yes.'

'This interview was during the proceedings before the magistrates?'

'Yes.'

'A bit odd, isn't it, to interview an accused person after proceedings have started?'

'He asked for the interview.'

'I dare say he did,' said Roger. 'But why did you give it him?'

'I wanted to know what he was going to say.'

'Maybe,' said Roger, 'but he was represented by solicitor and counsel, and so was the prosecution. Did you ask any superior officer or anyone from the Director of Public Prosecutions Office whether there was any objection to your having the interview?'

'I told the superintendent I was having the interview.'

'That isn't what I asked you. Did you ask anyone whether it would be proper for you to have the interview?'

'No.'

'Have you ever done such a thing before?'

'I don't think so.'

'Then why on this occasion?'

'I wanted to know what he was going to say.'

'Do you mean that you thought you might get some more evidence?'

'Possibly.'

'I suggest that you thought you might get some more money.'

'Nothing of the kind,' said the inspector indignantly.

'Why so indignant, inspector?' asked Roger. 'Did you think it more likely that the defendant was coming for a proper purpose or an improper purpose?'

'I didn't know.'

'Of course you didn't *know*, but did you think it more likely to be improper or proper? Here was a man who had already given you money and he asks to see you in the middle of a case. Pretty irregular, wasn't it?'

'I told him so,' said the inspector.

'I know you did,' said Roger, 'and that's why I ask the question again. Was it more likely for a proper or improper purpose? More likely is all I ask.'

The inspector hesitated for a moment. Then:

'Improper, I suppose,' he answered.

'In what way improper?' asked Roger.

Again the inspector hesitated.

'May I help you?' said Roger. 'Possibly he was going to try to bribe you again?'

'Possibly,' said the inspector.

'Then why were you so indignant a moment ago when I asked you if you thought you might get some more money?'

'I thought you meant for myself,' said the inspector.

'Why did you think that?' asked Roger.

'From the way you asked the question,' said the inspector.

'Any other reason?' asked Roger.

The inspector did not answer at once.

'Come, inspector,' said Roger, 'is it such a very difficult question? You say that you thought my question meant that you expected to get some money for yourself. Very good. Now, was there any other reason except my manner of asking the question which made you think that?'

Again there was a pause. Then the inspector said:

'What the defendant himself said, I suppose.'

'And what was that?'

'He said he'd given me more than I'd put in the charge sheet.'

'You mean,' said Roger, 'that he said to you that he had given you more money than you handed over to your superior and that you had dishonestly kept the balance for yourself? That was the effect of what he said, was it not?'

'Yes,' said the inspector.

'And what was your reply?' asked Roger.

Again the inspector hesitated.

'You were very indignant with me a moment ago,' said Roger. 'I suppose you were very indignant with Mr Glacier and denied his wicked lies?'

As there was still no answer, Roger went on:

'Come, inspector, didn't you deny what he said?'

'No,' said the inspector, 'I didn't get the chance.'

'Oh – why was that?' asked Roger – in an interested, inquiring tone.

'He said something else at the same time . . . and – and –'

'You fainted,' put in Roger, 'and banged your head?'

'Yes,' said the inspector.

'What else did he say?' asked Roger.

'He said that our conversation was being listened to by the Chief Constable and the superintendent.'

'Which was the greater shock?' asked Roger.

'I don't quite understand,' said the inspector.

'Was it a greater shock to be told that you'd kept some of the money or that the conversation was being tapped – or was it a combination of both?'

'I don't know,' said the inspector. 'I suppose it was both.'

'It was true that the conversation was being tapped, wasn't it?'

'Yes.'

'It was also true, wasn't it, inspector, that you'd kept some of the money?'

'It was not.'

'On neither occasion?'

'Certainly not.'

'But you didn't deny it to Mr. Glacier, did you?'

'I didn't get the chance.'

'You've heard the record of the conversation played over, haven't you?'

'Yes.'

'There was a pause between Mr Glacier's two questions, wasn't there?'

'There was a slight pause.'

'Why didn't you take advantage of it to deny the allegation?'

'It was a shock.'

'You mean that?'

'Yes.'

'But aren't you used to having accused persons making wicked and untrue allegations against you?'

'Sometimes.'

'It's quite frequent, isn't it?'

'It does happen.'

'Then why was it such a shock?'

'I can't say why exactly, but it was.'

'May I suggest as a reason,' said Roger, 'that you were so

surprised at Mr Glacier telling the whole truth about the matter?'

'No.'

'Didn't you think that he would deny ever having given you any money?'

'I didn't know what he would say.'

'Of course you didn't *know*, but didn't you *think* he would deny ever having given you any money? That's what you'd expect him to do, isn't it?'

'Possibly.'

'Well, of course, if he denies having given you any money he can't say he's given you more than you've handed over to your superiors, can he?'

'I suppose not.'

'So that, if you have been dishonest and if he's going to deny giving you any money, you're pretty safe, aren't you?'

'It didn't happen.'

'I didn't ask you if it happened,' said Roger. 'I asked if it seemed to you a pretty safe thing for a dishonest inspector to do?'

'I don't know whether it would be safe or not. I've never considered it.'

'I suggest,' said Roger, 'that you not only considered it but that you did it.'

'I did not.'

Roger then proceeded to put Mr Glacier's story about Melanie to the inspector. But he did not do it at any great length as it was a side of the story in which he did not have much faith.

Later the sergeant gave evidence, corroborating what the inspector had said in his evidence-in-chief. Roger then cross-examined him.

'You know P.C. Thrussle, do you not?' was his first question.

'Yes,' said the sergeant.

'An officer of good character?'

'As far as I know.'

'On quite good terms with you?' asked Roger.

'Yes – quite.'

'Any reason you can think of why he should tell a lie to injure you?'

'I can't think of any.'

'Do you meet him in the canteen sometimes?'

'Yes.'

'Chat about this and that?'

'Yes.'

'Ever speak to him about this case?'

'I told him we'd got it on.'

'Anything else about it?'

'Not that I remember.'

'Let me see if I can help you,' said Roger. 'Did you mention the amount that had been handed to the inspector?'

'I don't think so.'

'Didn't you? Just try to think.'

'It was only a casual conversation.'

'Drinking beer at the time?'

'I do drink it. Very likely I was then.'

'Tell me, sergeant, have you had any experience of bribery cases before?'

'I've had to do with one or two.'

'In each case the accused person denied he'd paid any money?'

'Yes.'

'That's what they usually do, isn't it?'

'I believe so.'

'That's what you'd expect them to do, isn't it?'

'I suppose so.'

'So that, if an officer wanted to be dishonest, he could keep part of the bribe for himself?'

'I suppose he could do.'

'Ever heard of such a thing being done?'

'No.'

'I suggest you have – and in this case too.'

'What d'you mean?'

Roger explained what he meant and the sergeant denied that anything of the kind had happened.

When the sergeant's evidence was completed, the superintendent gave evidence. He told of the inspector approaching him in the first instance, of the money being handed to him by the inspector on two separate occasions, and he produced the actual notes and the envelopes which had been opened by the magistrates' clerk. He was cross-examined by Roger about the trap set for the inspector, and he identified as correct a transcript taken from the record of the interview. He also gave evidence of finding the inspector on the ground.

'Would you have been surprised if the inspector had acted dishonestly?' asked Roger.

'Yes, I would,' said the superintendent.

'Very surprised?' asked Roger.

'Yes, very.'

'You were completely satisfied of his integrity?'

'Yes.'

'Then why set a trap for him?'

'That was not my responsibility.'

'I see,' said Roger. 'So you throw that on to the Chief Constable, do you?'

'All I say is that it was not my responsibility,' repeated the superintendent.

'Is the Chief Constable going to be called as a witness, do you know?'

'That is not my responsibility,' said the superintendent.

Roger profoundly hoped, from his own personal point of view, that the Chief Constable would not be called. But from his clients' point of view he had to try to prod the prosecution into calling him. 'Is my learned friend going to call the Chief Constable?' he asked.

'Certainly not,' said Henry. 'My learned friend can call him himself if he wishes.'

'Thank you,' said Roger. 'I will consider the invitation in due course.'

'Mr Thursby,' said the judge, 'I think it would be better if you confined your cross-examination to asking questions.'

'If your Lordship pleases,' said Roger.

Not long afterwards the case for the prosecution was closed and Roger opened the case for the defence. Among other things, he said :

'Members of the jury, I entirely agree with my learned friend that corruption is a deadly disease and I say at once – whether my clients like it or not – that if you are satisfied that my clients or either of them are guilty, they deserve no sympathy whatever. I also agree with my learned friend that our police force is the most reputable in all the world. We rely on them and they seldom let us down. But there must be an exception to the rule from time to time, and it is my duty to suggest to you, on behalf of my clients, that this case has uncovered one of them – the case, it might be called, of The Fainting Inspector. I will deal a little later with the circumstances which led up to his unfortunate accident. At the moment I will only remind you that you are not trying the inspector; you are trying my clients and if, in all the circumstances, you are not satisfied as to their guilt, that is an end of the matter and they are entitled to be acquitted. Now, in most cases of this kind the defence can only rely upon the evidence of the man or woman charged with the offence. In this case, fortunately for the defendants, I am in a position to call before you another police officer who has nothing to gain – indeed, perhaps a good deal to lose – by giving evidence for the defendants.'

Roger then went on to outline what the police constable would say and, when he had finished, he called Mr Glacier as his first witness. He took him through the whole of his story, of how grateful he was that his little Melanie had not been charged, of the circumstances in which he came to give money to the inspector, and of the amount he gave. Finally, he gave evidence of the interview with the inspector. Roger then sat down, and Henry got up.

'Are you an honest man, Mr Glacier?' he asked.

'Ah,' said Mr Glacier, 'what is honesty?'

'Well what do you call it?' asked Henry.

Mr Glacier put his hands on the witness box. 'This is an opportunity I have been waiting for. I have often envied the parson who, without fear of interruption or contradiction, can express his views to his congregation on all manner of subjects. Now –'

'Be quiet,' said the judge, 'and listen to me. You will give your evidence properly or not at all.'

Mr Glacier raised his eyebrows. 'I am sorry to have offended your Lordship. It was unintentional, I assure you.'

'Very well, then,' said the judge.

There was silence for a moment.

'Well?' said the judge. 'Are you going to answer counsel's question, or not?'

'My Lord,' said Mr Glacier, 'how do you wish me to answer it? I am asked a – how do you say? – a metaphysical question. How can I answer it except in the same – what is the word? – the same idiom? What is honesty? It is a big – a very big question. I could talk for hours on it. I assure your Lordship I will not do so,' he added hurriedly.

'I can assure you you won't,' said the judge. 'Mr Blagrove,' he added, 'it is rather a large question. Do you really need an answer? I fancy the jury can judge what is meant by honesty from the practical point of view.'

'If your Lordship pleases,' said Henry. 'Very well, then, Mr Glacier. Whatever you yourself mean by honesty, do you count yourself an honest man – as honest as the next man?'

'That rather depends upon who he is,' said Mr Glacier. 'I should expect to be in a higher class than Inspector Worcester.'

'Very well, then,' said Henry. 'Do you consider it honest to bribe the police?'

'Most assuredly not.'

'It is not a thing you would do?'

'It is most certainly not.'

'But you would give the police large sums of money?'

'I give the tax collector large sums of money, but I do not bribe him.'

'Do you think it proper to give the police money at all?'

'I have been thinking about this,' said Mr Glacier, 'since

these proceedings were started, and I realize now that I was wrong to give money at all. My motives might have been misunderstood – and, in fact, they have been grossly misrepresented. I shall not be so foolish again.'

'Then you now consider that you acted improperly?'

'Yes. I regret it. But it was not a crime.'

'It was not the crime with which you are charged,' said Henry.

The judge intervened. 'Mr Blagrove, if you consider that the defendants' own story discloses an offence against the Prevention of Corruption Act, why didn't the prosecution charge them with it? They are charged with giving money to procure a favour in the future. Why weren't they charged with giving money for a past favour?'

'I can tell your Lordship that at once,' said Henry. 'It seemed to the prosecution, rightly or wrongly, that, if the jury accepted the story put forward by the defendant – and rejected that of the police officers – it would not be right to ask for a conviction for a crime which no witness for the prosecution alleges took place.'

'I understand,' said the judge. 'That seems eminently fair.'

'If your Lordship pleases,' said Henry, and continued his cross-examination. He led up to the interview during the magisterial proceedings. 'Now tell me, Mr Glacier,' he said, 'why didn't you give the inspector the chance of answering your allegation about the money before you went on to tell him that the conversation was being tapped?'

'Oh, Mr Blagrove, if I had your knowledge of the art of cross-examination I might have acted differently,' said Mr Glacier.

'Mr Glacier,' said Henry, 'I do not propose to let you slip out of the question in that way. I consider it a very important one. Will you kindly deal with it seriously? Will you tell my Lord and the jury what possible object there could have been in telling the inspector about the interview being tapped before he answered the question about the money?'

'Sometimes,' said Mr Glacier, 'I have heard counsel ask

two questions in one sentence. Can I be blamed if I, a layman, do the same?'

'Mr Glacier, I suggest to you that you put the two questions quite deliberately – that you knew what the inspector's
answer would be to the first question and that you didn't
want him to give it until you'd shocked him by disclosing
about the tapping of the interview?'

'What is the question, please?' asked Mr Glacier. 'If I
may say so, there seem to be at least two questions in that
one. Even three perhaps.'

'Why did you want to disclose to the inspector that the
conversation was being tapped at that particular moment?'

'Why did I want to do that?' said Mr Glacier. 'I do not
know that I really did want to do it. I did it. I cannot say
why. It just happened. Like so many things. I repeat in all
seriousness that, if I had had your training, I might have
done it differently.'

Henry finished his cross-examination. Roger did not re-
examine, and called his next witness – Mrs Glacier. She said
what was expected of her by both sides, and then the police
constable was called. He stuck to his story, and though
Henry tried to see if he could trace any connexion between
him and the Glaciers, he was unable to do so. He swore
positively that the sergeant had told him that they had received altogether sixty-five pounds and were only putting
forty-five pounds in the charges; that he was frightened to
go to the superintendent and, not being prepared to leave
the matter undisclosed, he went to the Glaciers. Finally,
Roger called Mr Plumb to give evidence of his conversation
with the Chief Constable. The latter was in Court and his
anger was so great that he had some difficulty in refraining
from making an outburst. He reserved that for later. Digby
was sitting between Henry and Roger and, as Roger began
to ask the questions which would lead to a disclosure of what
the Chief Constable had said to Mr Plumb, he started a soft
obbligato accompaniment – 'in breach of confidence, in
breach of confidence, in breach of confidence.'

'Shut up,' said Roger.

'In breach of confidence,' repeated Digby.

'I wish you'd control your little yapper,' said Roger to Henry.

'In breach of confidence,' repeated Digby, 'and I shall go on saying it until you've finished.'

'Don't be an ass,' said Roger. 'Do muzzle him,' he said to Henry, adding, 'if you don't, I shall have to ask the judge to do so.'

'What is happening at the Bar?' asked the judge. 'It is most inconvenient for me and the jury to have this noise going on. Please continue with the evidence, Mr Thursby.'

Digby eventually subsided and a very unwilling Mr Plumb proceeded to state what the Chief Constable had said – namely, that he had suspected the inspector for a long time and would be damned glad to get him.

'How is this admissible?' asked the judge.

'My Lord,' said Roger, 'is it not material that a party to litigation who calls a witness to support his case does not believe in the honesty of that witness? Could not a plaintiff be asked such a question regarding his chief witness? And, if he could, is not the Chief Constable in the same position? I, of course, appreciate that the prosecution is by the Queen. But the Queen can only act through agents and, if a person who has been responsible for the conduct or initiation of the prosecution makes such a statement regarding an important witness, it must – in my respectful submission – be material for the consideration of the jury.'

'I see how you put it, but I'm not at all sure that it's right,' said the judge.

'If a plaintiff or the Director of Public Prosecutions said of a witness he is calling – "he is not a trusted servant of mine" – surely that would be a matter proper for the consideration of the jury?'

'You can't call affirmative evidence to show bad character,' said the judge.

'I respectfully agree,' said Roger, 'but the object of this evidence is to show that the prosecution, through its agent – the Chief Constable – has no belief in its case. Would it not be a proper question to ask a party to litigation who has called a witness to an important incident – "have you any belief that the incident really happened?" '

'I should have thought not,' said the judge. 'The belief of the plaintiff in his own witness has surely nothing to do with it. It is what the judge or jury thinks of the witness that matters. In so far as the matter goes to the credit of the witness, you must agree it is not admissible. And I must confess I can't see why the belief or disbelief of a plaintiff or Director of Public Prosecutions in the worthiness of a witness has anything to do with the matter. Obviously, if the Director knew anything specifically to the discredit of the witness, he would probably inform the defence of the matter. And, of course, the matter could be put to the witness in cross-examination.'

'My Lord,' said Roger, 'I respectfully submit that, in a criminal prosecution at any rate, the disbelief of the prosecutor – using that term in the sense I have mentioned – in the honesty of an important witness must be a matter for the consideration of the jury.'

'Well, what do you say, Mr Blagrove?' asked the judge.

'My Lord, whatever the strict legal position may be,' said Henry, 'I should not seek to exclude evidence which the defence desire to tender unless it is quite unarguable that it is inadmissible. I would respectfully agree with what has fallen from your Lordship, but, as I concede that there is an argument to be put forward in favour of the evidence being received, I do not ask your Lordship to reject the evidence.'

'Very well, then,' said the judge. 'In these circumstances I will say nothing more – except that I have grave doubts as to its admissibility.'

'As the question of admissibility has been raised,' said Roger, 'I think it only right to tell your Lordship that, after the Chief Constable had made the statement, he said to my client – "That's in confidence, of course," and my client said – "Of course." Now, as your Lordship may imagine, in those circumstances it is with the greatest regret and considerable embarrassment that I have felt bound to tender the evidence. If I could have avoided doing so, I should certainly have done so, but, if it is admissible in evidence, it seems to me that the defendants are entitled to the benefit of it. I hope your Lordship will think I have taken a proper course.'

'I am quite sure,' said the judge, 'that you have acted in accordance with your duty to your client. There can, of course, be no such thing as "without prejudice" conversations in criminal matters and, unfortunate though the matter is, it seems to me that, if the evidence is otherwise admissible, the Chief Constable's statement about confidence cannot have the effect of excluding it. Moreover, it seems to me that in a criminal matter different considerations apply from those which obtain in civil litigation. I do not think any other course was open to you.'

'I am very grateful to your Lordship,' said Roger, and hoped the Chief Constable was listening. He was.

'These lawyers always stick together,' he whispered to a friend in Court.

After Mr Plumb had completed his evidence, Roger addressed the jury – submitting to them that at the least the case for the prosecution had not been proved against either of his clients. Henry followed him on behalf of the prosecution and submitted that, on the contrary, the case had certainly been proved against Mr Glacier. As regards Mrs Glacier, if the jury thought she might have been under her husband's influence and was not a willing party to the bribery, he could not ask for a conviction against her. Finally, Mr Justice Kingsdown summed up. He reminded the jury of what the charges against each of the accused were; he spoke of the gravity of such charges, and then he went on :

'Now, members of the jury, in this country it is not for a prisoner to prove his innocence but for the prosecution to prove his guilt. Now, how must they prove that guilt? They cannot prove it with complete certainty – for you could only be completely certain of a prisoner's guilt if you not only were present at the commission of a crime but plainly saw it committed. In such a case you would be witnesses, not jurors. So you will see that justice could not be administered if complete certainty were required. But what is required is that the prosecution should prove the defendant's guilt with reasonable certainty. Suspicion is not enough – even strong suspicion. Before you can convict you must be reasonably sure that the Crown has made out its case. And when I say reasonably sure, you will understand – for the reason I have explained – that you cannot be expected to be completely sure. You must be reasonably sure. So much for the measure of proof. Now, what the prosecution have to prove with that measure of proof is this.'

The judge then explained the ingredients of the offence with which the defendants were charged.

'Whatever your view may be about the guilt or innocence of Mr Glacier, members of the jury,' he went on, 'you may well think that the case against Mrs Glacier has not been satisfactorily established. The law on the subject is as follows : there is no presumption that a wife acts under the coercion of her husband but, if the offence is committed by her in his presence, she may prove – if she can – that she was in fact acting under his coercion. If she does so she is entitled to be acquitted. The only evidence against Mrs Glacier is that she was present when the crime – if crime it was – was committed. She does not say her husband coerced her, but on the other hand it is his act that constituted the crime, and if she is liable it is only because he acted on her behalf. Now, in all the circumstances, are you reasonably sure that Mrs Glacier has committed any offence? If you are, you will, of course, find her Guilty; but you may think – it is entirely a matter for you – that it would be very dangerous on the evidence – and you are concerned with the evidence and the evidence alone – to find her Guilty of either of the charges against her. I need hardly say that, if you find Mr Glacier Not Guilty, you would, of course, find his wife Not Guilty also. But, up till now, I have dealt with the case of Mrs Glacier separately – in other words, even if you should find her husband Guilty, you may well take a different view of

the case against her. I will now come to the much more difficult problem before you – the question of Mr Glacier. Counsel has quite rightly told you that you are trying him and
not the inspector or the sergeant. That is absolutely true, but
it will be impossible for you to come to a conclusion about
the guilt or innocence of Mr Glacier without weighing up
the evidence of the inspector and the sergeant. If you think
they are a couple of scoundrels – that is an end to the
matter. But if you are satisfied of that, you still have to be
reasonably sure that what they are saying is substantially
true before you can return a verdict of Guilty. And in that
connexion you have to weigh up the evidence of the police
constable who gave evidence for the Glaciers.'

The judge then proceeded to go into the evidence in detail
and, when he had done so, he said :

'Well, members of the jury, that is what these witnesses
said. What do you believe to be the truth? If you are left in
a state of uncertainty, the defendants are entitled to be
acquitted. I have told you several times that, before you can
convict, you must be reasonably sure that the truth is in the
evidence given by the prosecution and not in that given by
and on behalf of the defendants. What kind of an impression
did the inspector and sergeant make on you? What kind of
an impression did Mr Glacier make on you? Did he appear
to you to be an honest man who was grateful to the police
for not charging his daughter – or did he appear to you to
be an extremely astute, exceptionally able man, who would
be quite capable of inventing a plausible story to get himself
out of his difficulties? It is of no importance what impression he made on me. What did *you* think of him? You may
think possibly that that is the crux of the matter. If the story
he is putting forward now is true, the inspector and sergeant are quite plainly wholly unfitted for their positions of
trust. But, if it is false, then it is difficult to resist the conclusion that the evidence of the police constable called on behalf
of the Glaciers is false also and – although there is no direct
evidence to show that he has been induced by the Glaciers
to give that false evidence – I think one must face that

position, and, personally, I do not see how that inference can be resisted *if*, and only if, the evidence of Mr Glacier is untrue in the material matters. There it is, members of the jury, you are the judges, not I. I have told you the law on the subject and that you must take from me. If I am wrong in any of my directions, I can be corrected elsewhere. But the facts are for you and for you alone. If anything I have said about the facts does not commend itself to you, disregard it. It is your views which matter, not mine. I do not think there is anything further I can usefully add, members of the jury, and I will ask you to consider your verdict. I expect you would like to retire.'

Chapter 21

MR GREEN

====

THE jury retired, and Roger and Henry were about to leave the Court while the next case was called – when a prisoner who wanted a dock brief was put in the dock.

'Has he two pounds four shillings and sixpence?' asked the judge.

'Yes,' said the clerk.

'Very well, then,' said the judge. 'You can choose any counsel you like.'

'Ah,' said the prisoner, whom Roger seemed dimly to recognize, 'but not one who's engaged on a case, can I?'

'No, that's quite correct,' said the judge, a little surprised. 'You seem to know all about it.'

'I've been caught before, my Lord,' said the prisoner, and then added hastily, 'about choosing counsel, I mean, my Lord. It's such a disappointment when you choose a really brainy-looking–'

'Now don't start making speeches,' said the judge. 'Choose someone.'

'All right, my Lord,' said the prisoner, 'I'll have him,' and pointed to Roger.

'You can't have Mr Thursby,' said the judge. 'He's engaged on a case.'

The prisoner looked plaintively at the judge. 'That's exactly what I meant, my Lord. It would be fairer if they had a label on them.' He paused for a moment and looked along the line of counsel : 'Some of them might have an L on them too, don't you think, my Lord?'

'Behave yourself,' said the judge.

'Did I hear you say Mr Thursby?' said the prisoner.

'I told you you can't have him,' snapped the judge.

Suddenly Roger realized who the prisoner was. He had

aged a good deal, but Roger recognized in him a Mr Green whom he had once defended successfully at the Old Bailey while he was still a pupil. In fact, Mr Green had done most of the defending and Roger had long ago come to the conclusion that Mr Green's idea of L-plates on pupils was not at all a bad one. They should not be allowed to appear except in company with an experienced practitioner who must sit next to them.

'My Lord,' said Roger, 'if it isn't too long a case, I'd be prepared to take it for the prisoner.'

'That's very good of you, Mr Thursby,' said the judge. 'Is it a long case, d'you know?' he asked. He was really addressing the clerk, but Mr Green took it on himself to reply.

'Nothing long about it,' he said and added, 'I hope.'

'Very well, then,' said the judge. 'Perhaps you'd like to see him now, Mr Thursby.'

'If your Lordship pleases,' said Roger. Before going to see his new client, he spoke to Henry. 'This is a chap I did a docker for when I was a pupil of Grimeyboy. I hope he'll think I've improved.'

'I gather he hasn't,' said Henry.

Roger went to see Mr Green. He certainly had aged, but there was still a good deal of the old sparkle Roger had noticed twelve years before.

'Nice to see you, Mr Thursby,' said Mr Green. 'Nice to see you any place, but I didn't come here for the purpose.'

'How are you?' said Roger. 'It is a long time ago. Things not too good since then?'

'Mustn't grumble,' said Mr Green. 'Lose good conduct marks if you do. Let me see,' and he thought for a bit. 'You were toffee, weren't you?'

'That's right,' said Roger, 'it was a case about toffee. Glad you got off. Sorry you're here now. What's it for?'

'Oh – don't let's spoil the party,' said Mr Green. 'Let's talk of something pleasant. Haven't seen you for years. We can't get a pint down here, I suppose?'

'I'm afraid not,' said Roger. 'We'll celebrate with one when we get you off.'

The old man – at any rate he now looked one – shook his head. His eyes grew a little moist. Then he brushed them with his hand in an impatient gesture. 'Come, come, Mr Green,' he said, 'pull yourself together. It's a long lane that has no turning. If you ask me,' he added, 'it's going to be a ruddy long lane this time.'

'What's it all about?' said Roger.

'I've lost my grip,' said Mr Green. 'I'm slipping. Slipped, you might say. Nice to see you again though. Takes me back a bit. Toffee. That was good fun. We had 'em on the run, didn't we?'

'You did,' said Roger. 'I just followed behind you.'

'Well – you've made up ground since then,' said Mr Green. 'See your name in the paper no end. Nice to be able to tell one's pals – "I started that young man off." I've had several beers on that.'

'Well, it's quite true,' said Roger, 'and you deserved them. As soon as I recognized you, I decided to accept the brief – that's, of course, if it was offered to me.'

'It's a shame,' said Mr Green, 'that there isn't more kick in it. We could have had a high old time together – you and me. If I'd known you were going to be here – I'd never have done it. I shouldn't have, anyway. I told you I'm slipping. D'you know what I've done?'

'No,' said Roger.

'I've admitted it,' said Mr Green. 'Can you beat it? Signed, sealed, and delivered on the dotted line. I-have-been-warned-that-anything-I-say-may-be-used-in-evidence-and-I-make-this-statement-voluntarily-after-having-been-cau-tioned-that-I-am-not-bound-to-say-anything-unless-I-wish-to-do-so. And what makes it worse is – that's quite true. I was warned. It was voluntary. No cigarettes or cups of tea. I go and make a ruddy voluntary confession. Can't think what I was up to. Tired, I suppose. I'll get four years this time. That means three nearly – if you don't grumble. Three years to wait for a pint of bitter. Hard, isn't it? Pity I'm not on bail. We could have popped across and had one.'

'If you're pleading Guilty, why did you want counsel? You know the ropes as well as anyone, I should say.'

'Thank you,' said Mr Green. 'Experience teaches. Yes, I do. But I don't know this judge. Never seen him, never read about him. I thought I'd better get a line on him. It's worth four years, but not a penny more. And suppose this chap doesn't know the scale, he might give me five or six even.'

'It cuts both ways,' said Roger. 'He might give you eighteen months.'

'Can't see it,' said Mr Green. 'Had three years last time. It's a good idea though. If they halved it each time instead of doubling it. I'd only get nine months next time. Only four and a half the time after. Hardly worth going in for. But what d'you think this is good for?'

'You haven't told me anything about it yet,' said Roger.

'There I go again,' said Mr Green. 'That's what I did with you last time. Can't make bricks without straw, the labourer is worthy of his hire, who sups with the devil needs a long spoon – now, where had I got to? Ah – the indictment. I used to call it in*dickt*ment until you told me how to pronounce it. I've always remembered since then. Funny how one doesn't notice these things. The clerk says in*dite*ment all right, but I'd never noticed till you told me. I won quite a few bets over that. Pity there's no beer down here. Sorry to run on. But bets always remind me of beer. They sort of go together.'

'Well, you'd better let me see it,' said Roger.

'The indictment?'

'Yes.'

'It's a scruffy-looking thing,' said Mr Green. 'Only two counts. But they'll be enough. Not so deep as a pint mug or as wide as a public bar – but they'll be enough – but I'll do the serving – worse luck.'

Roger looked at the charges against Mr Green, which were in substance that he had obtained one hundred and fifty pounds by pretending that he was running a genuine business called the Glenavon Chocolate Company.

'What was the total amount involved?' asked Roger.

'It says one hundred and fifty pounds there,' said Mr Green.

'I know,' said Roger.

'You are inquisitive,' said Mr Green. 'Do I have to tell you?'

'Not if you don't want to. But you might as well. The police will know. And it's better if I know what we've got to meet.'

'Well, as a matter of fact the business hadn't started long when something went wrong. I'm slipping, I tell you. I sent a man a cheque. If I'd just not paid him it'd have been all right. But I was feeling cocky. He'd written me a rude letter threatening all sorts of things. So I sent him a cheque.'

'And it bounced?'

'So high,' said Mr Green, and pointed to the ceiling. 'I hadn't an account, as a matter of fact, so you can't really blame the bank – though it was only for ten pounds and it wouldn't have hurt them to pay it. Still, there it is and here we are. What goes up must come down.'

'You haven't yet said how much is involved altogether.'

'Only about five or six hundred pounds. Hadn't had time to get started.'

'Don't you think you could get a decent job instead of this sort of thing?' said Roger.

'Now you've said something,' said Mr Green. 'That's what I say every time. To the judge too. I'll go straight, really I will. My Lord, if you will take a lenient view of this offence I promise you I'll never appear in the dock again.' He paused for a moment. Then he said : 'Tell me – how many times d'you think a chap can say that and still keep his self-respect?'

'It depends on the chap,' said Roger. 'But seriously, when you come out next time, why don't you settle down to something? After all, you're not making much of a success of this kind of thing, are you? You've had a good many beerless months in the last ten years, I should imagine.'

'You're quite right,' said Mr Green. 'I miss my beer and I've been without a lot of it, as you say. And I've had a bad season – too many bad seasons. Yes – you're quite right. But there's one trouble – and I don't know how you can get over that.'

'What is it?' said Roger.

'Well, between you and me,' said Mr Green, 'I don't like honest work.'

'It's lucky we're not all like that.'

'I certainly agree,' said Mr Green. 'It's very lucky indeed. Who'd run the trains and buses, who'd run Parliament, who'd run the Law Courts, the Stock Exchange, and so on and so forth? I can't really grumble, can I? I've lots of people working for me – the whole population nearly. And I get it all for nothing. Pretty good when you work it out that way.'

'Depends how long you have to enjoy it,' said Roger. 'When were you last inside?'

'Came out ten months ago. It was a Friday. Friday the thirteenth. That's a day to let you out. I suggested that in the circumstances they should make it the day before. They said they understood my feelings entirely and suggested the day after. So we compromised and I came out on the Friday.'

'Well, you'd better tell me something in your favour,' said Roger. 'How many honest days' work have you done in the last ten years?'

'I've just told you,' said Mr Green. 'I don't like it. Now, just listen. If I took a job – item – I'd have to work regular hours. Well – I just can't manage that. Then again you can't take holidays whenever you want to. You have people giving you orders. I'm not a Socialist, Mr Thursby. I don't believe that all men are equal or that everyone should have the same. Some people like being given orders. They wouldn't know how to run my business. They're happy in their little jobs. Start at nine, end at six. Half day Saturday. Fortnight's holiday a year. Christmas and Easter extra. Sounds lovely. So it is for them what likes it. I'm not one of them and I'm too old to start now.'

'Well,' said Roger, 'it's a change to have anyone so frank, but it won't be much use my telling the judge – that you'll do it again as soon as you come out and that you're not in the least sorry you've done it this time – only sorry you've been caught.'

'You don't think that would help?' said Mr Green. 'He wouldn't say – this fellow's so honest, he must have some good in him, and take off six months?'

'I doubt it,' said Roger. 'I doubt it very much. And the trouble is – now that you've told me that you've no intention of going straight and that you have never done so, I can't tell the judge the opposite.'

'Oh – I can change all that,' said Mr Green. 'I could put on an act, if you'd like me to. My Lord, I know I've done wrong, but I promise you –'

Roger interrupted. 'It won't do, I'm afraid,' he said. 'I can't deceive the judge.'

'No, of course not,' said Mr Green. 'It was very wrong of me to suggest it. I apologize, I withdraw, least said soonest mended, no broken bones, I hope.'

'Not at all,' said Roger. 'I'm glad we understand one another.'

'What would you advise then?' asked Mr Green.

'Well, quite frankly,' said Roger, 'I think you'd do better not to have counsel at all.'

'You advise me to make my own plea?' asked Mr Green.

'On the whole, I do,' said Roger.

'Do you realize,' said Mr Green, with a twinkle, 'that I shall try to deceive the judge?'

'You shouldn't do so, but I can't stop you,' said Roger.

'But you still advise me to make my own plea?' persisted Mr Green.

Roger did not answer at once, and Mr Green went on: 'Because, if that's so, you appear to be advising me to deceive the judge.'

'Certainly not,' said Roger. 'I advise you to tell him the truth.'

'What, and get an extra five years?' said Mr Green. 'Is that your best advice?'

'Perhaps not,' said Roger. 'You'd better say nothing at all.'

'But that won't do,' said Mr Green. 'He'll invite me to say something. And if I refuse – he'll fear the worst – and so shall I.'

'I don't see what else you can do.'

'Well, I do,' said Mr Green. 'I shall make an impassioned plea and promise that, if he exercises leniency, I'll never, never, never do it again. Never, never, never,' he rattled off quickly. 'Don't look so troubled. He won't be lenient and that lets me off the promise. Now, do you still advise me not to employ you?'

'I don't think there's anything I can do for you,' said Roger.

'Then, as they say upstairs,' said Mr Green, 'the answer is yes. But, as you know I'm going to tell a pack of lies to the judge, you're advising me to take a course which will result in the Court being deceived. How d'you get out of that one, Mr Thursby?'

'I don't know that I can,' said Roger. 'There's nothing whatever I can properly say in mitigation. So I'm bound to tell you that I can be no use to you. The result of that is that you'll defend yourself and I know that you'll lie in the process.'

'I suppose you couldn't get up in the middle when I'm saying my piece and tell the judge it's all lies.'

'Oh, good heavens, no,' said Roger. 'I couldn't do that.'

'I just wanted to be sure,' said Mr Green.

'Well, then,' he added, 'where do we go from here? Or perhaps that's a gloomy way of putting it. I think I'll solve your difficulty by withdrawing my instructions. That's the right expression, isn't it?'

'It is,' said Roger.

'Just before you go,' said Mr Green, 'tell me one thing for old time's sake. What's this judge like?'

'He's quite a good chap,' said Roger.

'Is he nice to young counsel?' asked Mr Green.

'Yes, very. Why do you ask?' said Roger.

'I just wondered,' said Mr Green. 'Now I suppose we'd better both get back,' he said. 'Look forward to our next meeting. Hope it won't be as long again – if it's in the right place,' he added.

Roger went back to Court and, at a convenient moment, Mr Green was put back in the dock. The jury in the Glacier case were still out.

'My Lord,' said Roger, 'the prisoner wishes to withdraw his instructions from me.'

'Very well,' said the judge. 'Do you wish to defend yourself then?'

'No,' said Mr Green, 'I'd like that one,' and he pointed to the white-wigged Mr Trent. The judge looked down at counsel's row and, for the first time, recognized his acquaintance of the races. 'Mr – ah – Mr –' he began.

'Trent,' said Mr Trent. 'Anthony Trent, my Lord.'

'Mr Trent, will you accept this brief?'

'I shall be very pleased, my Lord. I will go and see the prisoner at once and let your Lordship know as soon as I am ready to proceed.'

The judge resisted the impulse to inform him that he would kindly be ready for the Court when the Court was ready for him. Mr Justice Kingsdown thought it most important in all proceedings, but particularly in criminal matters, that a client should not think he had done badly because of any deficiencies in his counsel. If – as he sorely wanted to do – he bounced Mr Trent up and down before the case began, it would be difficult for the prisoner to feel that he would have a satisfactory trial. So he contented himself with saying: 'That is very good of you, Mr Trent.'

'Not at all, my Lord,' said Mr Trent. 'I am only too anxious to assist the Court.'

I must find out where this young man belongs, thought the judge, and pass a word to someone in his chambers. He could think of some judges – more choleric than he was – for whom Mr Trent might be fatal.

While Mr Trent was interviewing Mr Green, the jury in the Glacier case sent a note to the judge. In consequence, the defendants were put into the dock again and Roger, Henry, and Digby took their places in Court.

'I have had a note from the jury,' said the judge, 'to this effect. "We are agreed about the case of Mrs Glacier, but not about the case of Mr Glacier. It might help if your Lordship would repeat what you told the jury about the extent to which the case has to be proved by the prosecution." I propose to have the jury back and comply with their request, unless either of you have any submission to make on the subject.'

Henry and Roger shook their heads. So the jury came back into Court and the judge repeated to them at some length and in substantially the same words what he had said before. He added at the end: 'I hope that will solve your difficulties one way or the other.'

The jury retired again. The judge dealt with the next two cases, which were pleas of Guilty, and then Mr Trent returned to Court and informed the clerk that his case was a plea of Guilty too. The judge said he would take it at once.

'We must watch this,' said Henry to Roger.

Mr Green was brought into the dock. The two charges were read out to him.

'Do you plead Guilty or Not Guilty?' asked the clerk.

'Unfortunately, Guilty,' said Mr Green. 'I should have liked to have given my young counsel a chance to show what he's made of, but I must stick to the truth and, as I'm guilty, I must plead Guilty. I'm sure your Lordship would approve of that.'

'Be quiet,' said the judge. 'Your counsel will address me on your behalf.'

'I only wanted to show willing,' said Mr Green.

Counsel for the prosecution then outlined to the judge the facts of the case and called a police officer to state the character and antecedents of Mr Green. He also read out a list of his convictions. Mr Trent said that he had no questions to ask. That's something, thought the judge, but his optimism was premature.

'Yes, Mr Trent?' he said. 'Do you wish to say anything in mitigation?'

'If your Lordship pleases,' began Mr Trent. 'I will start

by reminding your Lordship of the duties of the Court in passing sentence. First of the matters you should consider generally and then of the matters you should consider by way of mitigating the offence and then – yes – of the matters, if any, of aggravation. These remarks of mine will, of course, be entirely general and by way of what I may term preliminary submission and will not be concerned with this case in particular.'

'I should prefer you to confine your remarks to this case, Mr Trent,' said the judge, with as little grimness as possible.

'Oh, my Lord,' said Mr Trent, 'I have not made myself plain. I am so sorry. Of course my remarks will be relevant – if I may say so, they will be highly relevant – they concern every case where a judge is passing sentence and therefore they cover this case as well. They are remarks of general application.'

'So I gather,' said the judge, 'but I have had some experience of the duties of the Court in this respect.'

'I'm quite sure your Lordship has,' said Mr Trent, 'but I feel that it might help your Lordship in approaching this case if I brought some of the more salient matters to your Lordship's attention. Now, my Lord, in the first place your Lordship should consider the nature of the actual crime committed. Let me take an example. Supposing a man with many previous convictions is charged with a really trivial offence –'

'Mr Trent,' said the judge, 'I really cannot allow you to take up the time of the Court by reminding me of things I already know and which have been established for years. Pray confine your remarks to this particular case.'

'Then your Lordship is bearing in mind,' said Mr Trent, 'that, having first considered the nature of the crime, the Court's next duty is to consider –'

'Mr Trent,' interrupted the judge, with some heat, 'you have not been very long at the Bar and I am afraid you have a lot to learn.' The judge paused – not because he had finished but because he was saying to himself – you must tone it down, you simply must, or that wretched chap in the dock will think he's got an extra year because you didn't see eye to eye with his counsel. This gave Mr Trent the chance of saying :

'Indeed I have, my Lord. And might I say that I am most grateful to your Lordship for any instruction your Lordship sees fit to give me.'

This gives me a chance, thought the judge, but, before he could say anything, Mr Trent went on :

'Of course, I'm sure your Lordship will understand that I am here to act solely in the interests of my client, as I see them, and, supposing any advice your Lordship should very kindly give me should happen not to coincide with views I have formed after mature consideration – views, I frankly admit, which may be wrong – but I can only act on what I think right, for better or worse, can I not, my Lord –'

Something burst on the Bench.

'Mr Trent, be quiet and listen to me. When you are in my Court, you will do as I say. If you object to any of my rulings, you can go to the Court of Criminal Appeal.'

'Is your Lordship giving me leave to appeal?' asked Mr Trent blandly.

I can't stand much more of this, thought the judge. 'There is nothing to appeal from at the moment, Mr Trent,' he said with some difficulty.

'That's why I didn't follow your Lordship's observation,' said Mr Trent.

Never in his career had Mr Justice Kingsdown wanted to take off his wig and throw it at counsel, and to follow it up with the glass and bottle of water which were by him – and after that to run yelling blue murder through the streets, or to sit sobbing in his private room. 'This is intolerable,' he said. He had not meant to say it aloud, but it slipped out.

Mr Trent looked puzzled. Then a light dawned on him. 'Usher,' he said in a low voice, but one that could be heard, 'Usher – open some windows. His Lordship is finding the heat intolerable.'

'Mr Trent,' said the judge, in his sternest voice, 'are you intending to be funny?'

'Funny, my Lord?' said Mr Trent, 'certainly not, my Lord. I heard your Lordship say that something was intolerable and I could only imagine it was the heat, my Lord.'

'It was not the heat, Mr Trent – it was you,' said the judge. Again he had not meant to say it aloud, but he simply could not restrain himself.

'Me, my Lord?' said Mr Trent, in a surprised voice. 'I'm so very sorry, my Lord. Could your Lordship perhaps be kind enough to tell me what I have done to offend your Lordship, and then – subject, of course, to my client's interests – I will do all I can to remedy the matter.'

'Mr Trent,' said the judge, as calmly as possible, 'you can best remedy the matter by saying as shortly as possible what there is to be said on your client's behalf in mitigation of sentence.'

'But that's what I was doing, my Lord. No doubt, owing to my inexperience, I was doing it clumsily and not probably as your Lordship, when in my position, used to do it – but I do assure your Lordship that I am trying and trying only to urge on my client's behalf the various matters which are in his favour. But, in order to do that, it is necessary – in my view – and here I am sure your Lordship will forgive me if I cross swords with your Lordship –'

'Mr Trent,' said the judge, 'sit down.'

Mr Trent, looking puzzled, remained standing.

'Sit down, Mr Trent, sit down, sit down, sit down. If you don't, I will have you removed by the usher.'

Mr Trent, quite bewildered, did as he was told.

'Arthur Green,' said the judge, 'the sentence of the Court is that you go to prison for eighteen months.'

Mr Green seemed stunned by the sentence at first – and then he turned to his attendant warders. 'Quick,' he said in a whisper, 'down the stairs before he changes his mind.'

Mr Trent was soon able to tell his friends – and others – that he got off an old lag with eighteen months after he'd only recently come out from doing three years for a precisely similar offence. And, indeed, the leniency was entirely due to Mr Trent. Mr Justice Kingsdown had ensured that the prisoner would not think that he had received a heavier sentence because of his counsel and that, although he had refused to listen to a speech in mitigation, the sentence he passed was not one which the Court of Criminal Appeal would reduce. Indeed, had Mr Green appealed they would doubtless have increased it. But there was to be no appeal by Mr Green, who went to gaol almost singing. 'And what pleases me so much,' he wrote to Roger, 'and what I am sure must please you, is that we were able to affect his Lordship's mind without telling any lies or making any promises.'

Chapter 22

THE VERDICT

━━━

EVENTUALLY the jury returned to Court, agreed. They acquitted Mrs Glacier, but they convicted her husband. Roger was surprised. Mr Glacier was extremely displeased. The Chief Constable was slightly – only slightly – mollified. The judge sentenced Mr Glacier to nine months' imprisonment. Roger and Mr Plumb interviewed him after he had been sentenced.

'Mr Glacier,' said Roger, 'I think you should appeal. In my view the judge's summing-up was wrong in law in one important respect.'

'You will understand, Mr Thursby,' said Mr Glacier, 'that I do not place entirely the same confidence in your views. I do not mean by that that I think you conducted my defence badly. Nothing of the kind. I think your cross-examination of the inspector was – how do you say? – a masterpiece. But I should have enjoyed it more if I had been acquitted. No – I am grateful to you for your conduct of the case. But you will remember that you told me that I had a good chance of being acquitted.'

'So you had,' said Roger, 'and the jury took long enough to arrive at their verdict.'

'Not as long as nine months,' said Mr Glacier. 'But there,' he added, 'I must not yield to despair. I still have confidence in your ability. Is there really a chance of success in the Appeal Court?'

'Definitely,' said Roger. 'It's not altogether an easy Court, but I think you've a good point and, even if you lose there, I think there's a very good chance of your being able to get to the House of Lords. It's a point of great public importance, in my view.'

'And will it take more than nine months to get to the House of Lords?' asked Mr Glacier.

'It certainly won't,' said Roger, 'but, even if it did, it would surely be worth your while to get rid of the conviction, even if you've served the sentence. And it's possible that, if the appeal took a long time, you'd get bail.'

'I must leave it to you and Mr Plumb,' said Mr Glacier. 'If you think I should appeal – very well, be it so. But may I say that I trust you will be as quick over the matter as possible?'

'We shall lose no time,' said Mr Plumb mournfully. 'I'm so very sorry about it. Perhaps Mr Thursby would settle a notice of appeal at once. Meanwhile Mr Glacier and I had better discuss arrangements for his business and his wife – during his . . . absence.'

Roger left Mr Plumb and Mr Glacier together and then went to look for Anne. 'D'you think,' he asked her, very soon after he had found her, 'that it would be any good my seeing your father?'

'Not at the moment,' she said. 'I must say . . . I see his point of view.'

'You don't mean you agree with it?' he asked unhappily.

'Well – I don't know,' said Anne. 'I haven't really met any lawyers before, and I don't know their standards.'

'That's a horrid thing to say,' said Roger. 'It means you think I played a dirty trick on your father. I've done nothing of the kind. In the first place, I had no idea Glacier would give the show away at the interview with the inspector.'

'You used something father told your solicitor in confidence,' said Anne.

'I couldn't help doing so. I didn't want to – but I had to. The judge said I acted perfectly properly.'

'Yes, I know,' said Anne. 'Father told me.'

'Well, doesn't that make any difference?' he asked.

'Father says you all stick together – and that's true I suppose . . . like doctors and all professional men.'

'If you mean that a judge would say something was proper when it wasn't – just because he wanted to help a member of the Bar – that's absolutely untrue. He might say nothing, but he certainly wouldn't give his blessing to something he thought wrong.'

'Well, I'm glad you didn't do anything improper then,' said Anne. 'But you can't expect me to fall on your neck and kiss you for breaking a confidence. I think it's terribly important to be able to trust people.'

'So do I,' said Roger. 'Don't you trust me?'

'Well – ought I to after what you've just told me? Suppose I told you something in confidence now – and it became useful to you to use it for a client of yours – I shouldn't feel very safe with my confidences.'

'That would be quite different,' said Roger. 'That would have been learned privately . . . not in the course of acting for a client. Why can't you look at it from my point of view? Suppose you were acting for someone who was charged with murder, wouldn't you feel bound to use any material you had which might show that they weren't guilty?'

'Well, that would include my private confidences,' said Anne, 'wouldn't it? So I'm not really safe in telling you anything.'

'It couldn't happen like that,' said Roger. 'There's no reasonable chance that it could happen.'

'But if it did, could I trust you?' asked Anne.

'If you refused to allow me to use the information, I don't suppose you could really. If you'd told me something in the strictest confidence – privately, nothing to do with any case – which later showed that a client of mine hadn't committed a crime – and if I asked you to let me use the information and you refused . . . I suppose that I should have to use it. And so would most people, I think. Which is the worse – to break your confidence or let a man whom you know to be innocent go to gaol or be hanged? Which do you think?'

Anne did not answer immediately, and Roger followed it up with : 'Well, suppose it was your problem . . . suppose you could save someone's life by breaking a confidence. Would you do it – or not?'

'Well, I must admit that the loss of a life is more important than the breaking of a promise.'

'Well, then, what's the difference in principle between death and prison? Prison might kill a man. It is very likely to ruin him and his family. If he's a claustrophobic it might send him mad. What would you do? If you could save an innocent man from prison by breaking a confidence – would you do it?'

'Mr Glacier wasn't innocent.'

'Oh come, Anne, that won't do – really. He's presumed innocent until he's found guilty. He's only guilty now because the jury think he was.'

'You argue very well, Roger,' said Anne. 'I'm not surprised you've done as well as you have.'

'But what I say is right,' said Roger, 'it really is. Don't let it come between us – whatever your father thinks about me.'

'I do see your point of view,' said Anne. 'I'll see what I can do with father. But he'll be a tougher nut to crack than I was ... but then, of course, that's rather different. I –' she trailed off.

'If only I've convinced you,' said Roger.

'I think you have,' said Anne, 'and I must say I didn't really want to win this argument.'

Chapter 23

COURT OF CRIMINAL APPEAL

═══

NOT long afterwards the case came before the Court of Criminal Appeal – consisting of Mr Justice Short, Mr Justice Rose, and Mr Justice Mellow. In opening the case to the Court, Roger, after a few preliminary remarks, said :

'My Lords, there is only one point in this appeal – a point of law but, in my submission, it is a very important one. This was a case where the jury took a considerable time to arrive at a verdict and, not only that, they expressly asked the judge to repeat his direction on what was the measure of proof required.'

'I have yet to learn,' said Mr Justice Short, 'that it is a ground of appeal that the jury took a long time to find the prisoner guilty.'

'It isn't,' said Roger, 'but if your Lordships will be good enough to hear what the ground of appeal is, I think your Lordships will find that the fact that the jury took a long time to arrive at a verdict is at least relevant in this case – though it is in no way essential to my appeal.'

'I don't know what your point is,' said Mr Justice Rose, 'but we've read the evidence. The jury obviously believed the evidence for the prosecution and not that for the defence. What's wrong with that?'

'Nothing, my Lord,' said Roger, 'if they were properly directed. I don't dispute that the jury were entitled to take the view they took if the summing-up of the learned judge was right in law.'

'Hadn't you better take us to the passages you complain of?' said Mr Justice Mellow. 'I'm bound to say it seemed to me a clear and admirable summing-up and not at all unfavourable to your clients.'

'My Lords,' said Roger, 'the misdirection of which I respectfully complain consists entirely of the way in which the learned judge directed the jury as to the burden of proof.'

'He said it was on the prosecution, didn't he?' asked Mr Justice Short. 'That's right, isn't it?'

'Yes,' said Roger, 'the learned judge said it was on the prosecution but, in my submission, he directed them wrongly about the extent to which the case had to be proved. It was because that is the sole point in this case that I ventured to draw your Lordships' attention to the importance which the jury apparently attached to this question of the onus of proof. That shows that – if there had been a different direction – they might have returned a different verdict.'

'If the learned judge had told the jury to acquit Mr Glacier, as he in effect told them to acquit Mrs Glacier, they might have found both of them Not Guilty, you mean?' said Mr Justice Short.

'No, my Lord, I don't mean that,' said Roger.

'Well, what is your complaint?' said Mr Justice Mellow. 'You concede that there's nothing wrong with the trial and nothing wrong with the summing-up, except this question of onus of proof. And the learned judge said it was on the prosecution. What more do you want? Didn't he say it often enough? Is that your complaint?'

'No, my Lord. My complaint quite simply is that, instead of saying that the jury must be satisfied beyond all reasonable doubt –'

'That's gone since *Summers*'s case,' said Mr Justice Mellow.

'In my submission, my Lords, it has come back since *Hepworth*'s case,' said Roger. 'But, even if I am wrong about that, the learned judge did not follow *Summers*'s or *Hepworth*'s case. He told the jury they must be reasonably sure of the defendants' guilt. In my submission, that is not enough. In *Hepworth*'s case this Court at least suggested that "satisfied" is not enough.'

'Well, what should he have said?' asked Mr Justice Rose. 'I see that he did say that complete certainty was impossible and was not required. That's right, isn't it?'

'Yes, my Lord,' said Roger.

'Well, if you can't have complete certainty,' said Mr Justice Short, 'what can you have but reasonable certainty?'

'That is not the expression used in *Summers*'s case, my Lord,' said Roger. 'The word used there is "sure" without qualification. The jury must "feel sure". That is repeated in *Hepworth*.'

'What do you say "sure" means?' asked Mr Justice Short.

'Frankly, I don't know,' said Roger. 'If "sure" means "sure" – it means "completely sure", which I agree is too high a standard. If it means something less than completely sure – how much less? I frankly don't know. But I do submit that the expression "reasonably sure" is putting it much too low. I'm reasonably sure I brought my watch with me means there may be quite a substantial element of doubt about it. With the greatest respect, my Lord, juries seem to have understood for many, many years the expression "satisfied beyond all reasonable doubt", and I should have thought that it was easier to explain that expression – if it requires explanation – than to explain what "being sure" or "feeling sure" means. I am sure I am addressing your Lordships. Have the jury to be as sure as that? No. Well, how far have they to be sure? If you tell a jury that they haven't to be absolutely sure but that they must be satisfied beyond all reasonable doubt – surely that tells them satisfactorily what is required?'

'I'm sure I brought my pen with me,' said Mr Justice Mellow reflectively, 'may mean ... I'm beginning to have some doubt whether I brought it with me.'

'I respectfully agree,' said Roger.

'Reasonably sure,' said Mr Justice Short, 'does sound more like the balance of probabilities. Crime has to be proved with a high degree of certainty. How that is to be defined, I'm not sure; but reasonably sure does appear to me, on reflection, to be putting the standard too low.'

'And,' put in Mr Justice Rose, 'this was – as Mr Thursby has pointed out – a case where the jury were troubled about the onus of proof. And they were told more than once – that they must be reasonably sure. That doesn't seem enough to me.'

'I think we'd like to hear what your opponent has to say,' said Mr Justice Short.

Henry began at once to address the Court.

'My Lords, I respectfully agree that, if this appeal had come before your Lordships twenty-five years ago, I should have found it difficult to support the learned judge's direction. But in the last ten years the Lord Chief Justice has more than once said that he thought the expression "satisfied beyond all reasonable doubt" was only calculated to muddle a jury or, at any rate, that an explanation of it had that effect.'

'It seems to have served satisfactorily for a good many years,' interposed Mr Justice Mellow.

'And in *Summers*'s case,' went on Henry, 'this Court approved the views of the Lord Chief Justice and said that that direction should not be given – and that the jury should be told that they should be satisfied of the prisoner's guilt so that they could feel sure their verdict was a right one.'

'I agree that the Court said that,' said Mr Justice Rose, 'but was it more than a strong intimation of the Court's views? It wasn't essential to the decision, was it? Moreover, in *Hepworth*'s case this Court said that *Summers*'s case may have been misleading and that the expression "beyond all reasonable doubt" would do. They also suggested that "satisfied" might not be enough.'

'That may be, my Lord,' said Henry, 'but there was *Kritz*'s case in 1949, where this Court expressly upheld a direction by a judge that the jury must be reasonably satisfied of the prisoner's guilt. With respect, there is no difference between "reasonably satisfied" and "reasonably sure".'

'How is that to be reconciled with *Hepworth*?'

'I doubt if it can be,' said Henry – 'although it was quoted to the Court during *Hepworth* and is mentioned in the judgment. But *Kritz*'s case was a definite decision, not a mere expression of opinion and, if "reasonably satisfied" has been held to be good, I submit that "reasonably sure" is just as good.'

'We'd better look at that decision then,' said Mr Justice Short. A copy of the report was obtained for each of their Lordships, and Henry read it to them.

'That is in your favour,' said Mr Justice Mellow, 'but I'm bound to say for myself that I don't think it's a very satisfactory direction. But that case was a much stronger case from the prosecution's point of view than this one.'

Mr Glacier listened to all these arguments, in the place specially provided for appellants in the Court, attended by two warders. He found the arguments not uninteresting, but the result of success or failure was so important to him that he wished it didn't take so long to arrive at it – provided, of course, that the result was favourable. At last, after Henry had addressed the Court at length and Roger had replied, the judges conferred together for a little time and then Mr Justice Short proceeded to give judgment.

'The appellant in this case,' he began, 'was convicted at Carpshire Assizes of two offences under the Prevention of Corruption Act 1906, and sentenced to nine months' imprisonment. He appeals against the conviction. The evidence at his trial was as follows.'

The judge then went into the evidence in some detail. Mr Glacier who, in the short time he had spent in prison, had learned to be able to speak without noticeably moving his lips, whispered very quietly to one of the warders : 'How long does this go on for? We all know the facts. What we want to know is the decision.'

'Don't worry, cock,' said the warder, who, as a result of his prison experience, had become an amateur ventriloquist. 'You're O.K.'

'They allow the appeal, you mean?' said Mr Glacier.

'Thumbs up,' said the warder.

'Can I go now, then?' asked Mr Glacier.

'Better wait till he's finished. They like you to do that.'

'Certainly, if you say so,' said Mr Glacier.

'Thanks, mate,' said the warder.

Meanwhile, Mr Justice Short was concluding his statement as to the evidence. He then dealt with the judge's summing-up, with the return to Court of the jury and the repeated direction given to them by the judge. He then stated what the ground of appeal was and elaborated the arguments for and against it.

'Personally,' he said, 'with the greatest respect to the learned Lord Chief Justice, I have always thought that the expression "satisfied beyond all reasonable doubt" was an admirable one – and it has served its purpose very well for many years. It is quite true that some judges have attempted to explain it at length and, in doing so, it is possible that they have confused the jury. But I can only say for myself that, if you tried to explain the extent to which a jury has to feel sure – having told them that they do not have to be completely sure – it would be just as easy to confuse them. Whereas, if you say to a jury – "you have not to be completely satisfied as to the prisoner's guilt, but there must be no real doubt in your minds about it, or, as we put it, you must be satisfied beyond all reasonable doubt," I should have thought a jury would have understood its duty well enough. On the other hand, if you use the expression "sure", I suppose you would have to say – "you must be as sure of the prisoner's guilt as you can be sure of anything which you have not plainly seen for yourselves." That may be putting the onus too high and *Summers*'s case does not say that. But it does say that a judge should tell the jury they must feel sure. I ask myself "how sure?" Whatever "sure" may mean – bearing in mind that, as it does not mean "absolutely sure", it does not really mean what it says – because "sure" means "absolutely sure" – unless it is qualified by some other word – I say again, whatever the expression may mean –'

'For how long does this continue?' asked Mr Glacier.

'You'll get away in time to have lunch at the Ritz,' said the warder.

'You will lunch with me, please?' said Mr Glacier.

'Can't, mate, thanks,' said the warder. 'Got to look after some more of you blokes.'

'Perhaps if I explained,' said Mr Glacier.

'You'd get six months for contempt,' said the warder.

'You must come and see me at my hotel then . . . the Glorious at Westlea. And bring your wife and family. I assume you have one.'

'Thanks, cock,' said the warder. 'But once you're out you'll forget all about me.'

'There you are wrong,' said Mr Glacier. 'I never forget a face or a friend.'

'There's no need to be personal,' said the warder – who had kind brown eyes but a large bulbous nose and a wart on the side of it.

'Forgive my English,' said Mr Glacier. 'I meant you are a friend – unless you are wrong about this appeal.'

'Don't you worry,' said the warder. 'I don't know nothing about the law. But you get to know what's happening when you've listened as often as I have.'

They stopped for a moment as the judge said : 'I say again – whatever that expression may mean, it is not the expression the learned judge used in this case.'

'He rests still at the same place,' said Mr Glacier.

'That's nothing,' said the warder. 'I've heard 'em at the same place all day, and then I've known 'em go on till the next.'

'Are you talking?' said the judge suddenly to Mr Glacier.

'No, my Lord,' said Mr Glacier, with the most innocent look on his face which he could produce.

'Well, someone was,' said the judge.

'It was him,' said the warder to Mr Glacier.

Mr Justice Short looked severely at the prisoner and continued with his judgment.

'His name's Short,' said the warder. 'Makes you smile.'

'Are they all like this?' asked Mr Glacier.

'Pretty well,' said the warder. 'But there are a few who say what the result is first, and give their reasons after. I think that's a bit fairer on the chap.'

'I collaborate, as my wife would say,' said Mr Glacier. 'It

is good to think I shall be seeing her soon. You are right, I suppose? Let me see where he is now.'

'Now the expressions which the judge used ...' Mr Justice Short was saying, 'were as follows –'

'No danger of him exceeding the speed limit,' said the warder. 'They don't, by the way. I used to be in the police force. And I've followed one old judge all down Constitution Hill and all along Birdcage Walk – twenty miles an hour exactly. Never more.'

'Perhaps he knew you were behind him,' said Mr Glacier. 'I should do the same in those circumstances.'

'Now, I wonder,' said the warder. 'I'd never thought of that.' He thought for a moment or two, which allowed Mr Glacier to hear Mr Justice Short say :

'Now, these expressions are not to be found in *Summers*'s or *Hepworth*'s case.'

'But I don't think so,' went on the warder. 'I bet these old geysers stick to the law. It stands to reason. Dishing it out all day – wouldn't be able to do anything else.'

'But, as a change, do you not think?' said Mr Glacier. 'It must be so very – how do you say? – boring to keep to the law all the time.'

'You wouldn't know, chum, would you?' said the warder.

'That might be described, I suppose, as a leading question,' said Mr Glacier. 'Whatever that expression may mean.'

'Whatever that expression may mean,' went on Mr Justice Short – and for a moment Mr Glacier's heart went at double time.

'I thought he had heard me again,' he said, after he had recovered.

'The one that's talking can't usually hear because of his own voice,' said the warder. 'And the ones that aren't are so busy listening to what's wrong with what the one that's talking says that they can't hear anything else. Or else', he added, 'they're asleep. With their eyes open, of course. That's one of the first things they learn on the Bench. Same as you learn to talk with your mouth shut in clink.'

'How do you know they sleep?' asked Mr Glacier, 'if their eyes are open?'

'By what happens when they wake up,' said the warder. 'They don't actually yawn and stretch themselves. But they'd like to. You can see 'em. Look at *him* now.'

He pointed to Mr Justice Mellow. 'Why shouldn't he have a bit of shut eye? He's got nothing to do now,' the warder added.

'Then will he not speak as well?' asked Mr Glacier.

'Shows you haven't been before, chum,' said the warder. 'Only one of 'em speaks. Even if they disagree. But then the one that disagrees – he keeps awake listening to all the mistakes the other two have made. There, he's waking up ... did you see that?'

Mr Justice Mellow had taken a glass of water.

'I expect he thought it was a cup of tea,' the warder added. 'Given him a nasty shock, look.'

They stared at Mr Justice Mellow sipping his water and imagined that they saw his Lordship give the suspicion of a jerk to his head.

'He nearly said : "What's the weather like, dear?" ' said the warder. 'But he's an old one. He was able to check it. They do say that before my time one of them did say something like it, but don't take it from me. I didn't hear it myself.'

'For myself,' said Mr Justice Short, 'I should be well satisfied to have left matters as they were before *Summers*'s case. But, even accepting that case, I do not think that the direction in the present case can be upheld. Does "reasonably sure" mean more or less than "almost sure?" "Almost sure" would not satisfy *Summers*'s case and "reasonably sure," if it is a stronger expression than "almost sure" – which I take leave to doubt – is certainly well below the standard of certainty required by "sure." '

'You are sure, I hope,' said Mr Glacier. 'Not almost sure?'

'Beyond all reasonable doubt, cock,' said the warder. 'It's about the only expression I know, but I've heard it so often it's stuck.'

'Completely and absolutely sure?' demanded Mr Glacier.

'As sure as he'll go on for another half hour,' said the warder.

'It is quite true,' went on Mr Justice Short, 'that in the case of *Kritz* cited by Mr Blagrove, this Court did dismiss an appeal where the judge had used the expression "reasonably satisfied". That case appears to us to be somewhat inconsistent with the later case of *Hepworth,* but, whether it was rightly or wrongly decided, it does not compel us to decide in this case that the repeated use of "reasonably" by the judge was a sufficient direction.'

'You seem to be right,' said Mr Glacier.

'Of course I'm right,' said the warder. 'Have you booked your table?'

'But why does he still continue?' asked Mr Glacier. 'He has said everything necessary to let me go.'

'Now Mr Blagrove has argued,' went on Mr Justice Short.

'He did not appear to argue as long as you,' said Mr Glacier who – though now very optimistic – was becoming impatient.

'Keep cool, chum,' said the warder. 'He's going to say it all – whether you like it or not.'

'So it seems,' said Mr Glacier.

'Some of 'em say it more than once,' said the warder.

'I have already gathered as much,' said Mr Glacier.

Almost exactly half an hour after the warder had said that it would go on for another half hour, Mr Justice Short paused for a moment and then said : 'For these reasons, we are all of opinion that the appeal must be allowed and the conviction quashed.'

The judge then looked towards the prisoner. 'Let him be discharged,' he said.

Mr Glacier bowed to the Court.

'This way, chum,' said the warder, but when he let him out below the Court to freedom and shook hands – 'Goodbye, sir,' he said, 'and good luck.'

'And good luck to you,' said Mr Glacier. 'We shall meet again.'

'Not here, I hope, sir,' said the warder.

'You may be sure beyond all reasonable doubt that it will not be here,' said Mr Glacier. 'Thank you for making the time pass much faster than it would otherwise have done. If only that judge would come for a drink to my hotel on a really thirsty day, after a long round of golf, I should take the place of the barman – and I should mix the drink myself. First I should fetch the ice – lovely cool ice – the basis of the beautiful drink that the judge is going to have. I should put it in the mixer with a few polite remarks about the weather and what a thirsty day it is. Then I should find that each ingredient had to be fetched from the cellar. And when I had them, I should pour them in so slowly – oh, so slowly. All the time I should make polite conversation – always about the weather – and thirst – and what a difference a long, cool drink makes; no doubt about it, I should say … no doubt about it. And then, when at last I had the beautiful mixture all ready and the judge's throat is in that most exquisite state of – how do you say? – of anticipation, when there is the certainty that the thirst is going to be – what is the word? – slaked … certainty, did I say? – perhaps I should have said reasonable certainty – then, at the last moment I should, by an unfortunate accident, drop the mixer and have to start all over again. First, of course, by clearing the mess – so very slowly.'

'I think that'd be a bit unkind,' said the warder. 'After all, he did let you off.'

'But so should I let him have his drink,' said Mr Glacier, 'in the end.'

Mr Glacier met Roger and Mr Plumb in the Law Courts and thanked them for their help. 'But what a lot of time and money,' he said, 'it has cost to arrive at the truth.'

'The truth?' said Roger. 'No one in Court said anything about arriving at the truth.'

Chapter 24

SILK

For a variety of reasons there was unusual delay in the appointment of Q.C.s but, not long after the successful end to the Glacier case, the Lord Chancellor intimated to Roger that he was recommending Her Majesty to appoint him one of her counsel learned in the law. In due course, the necessary ceremony took place and both Roger's mother and Anne came to see him take silk. They saw the silks, one after the other, come to the Law Courts from the House of Lords and assemble to have some photographs taken in their glory – full-bottomed wig, silk gown, Court dress, ruffle, and the rest – and then go round to most of the Courts where the ceremony of calling within the Bar took place. When each judge was told that the new Q.C.s had arrived, he stopped the case he was trying and, one by one, he called them within the Bar.

Roger had explained to his mother a year before what it was all about, but he told her again. ' "Moving the Court" is, in effect, making an application to the Court,' he said. 'And when you take silk, the judge always asks you, as a matter of courtesy, "Do you move?" – which means, have you any application to make. To show that you are now a Q.C., he is inviting you, as a pure formality, to do something in your new capacity. Of course no one has any application to make, and you simply bow – which is the method of saying "No".'

'But suppose you wanted to make an application?' Mrs Thursby asked.

'You'd make it another time, mother. This is just a ceremony. I don't know what would happen if anyone taking silk proceeded to get up, when he was asked if he moved, and launch a motion. The judge would have a fit.'

'Then don't you, Roger,' his mother said. 'It would be very unkind.'

'I won't, mother.'

In due course Roger's turn came and he duly took his place, gave the necessary bows, and sat down.

'Do you move, Mr Thursby?' said the judge.

Roger bowed, went along the row, and left the Court.

The ceremony took a long time – nearly all day – but it was over at last and Roger felt a free man. They celebrated the event by having a dinner at which all the members of his chambers were present.

The next day he celebrated the occasion again by taking Anne out to dinner and, after dinner, they went back to his mother's house. She had quite enough sense to go to bed early.

'Anne,' said Roger, and stopped. It was not as easy to say as he had thought. Perhaps she would help him. She did.

'Mr Thursby,' she said, 'do you move?'

Roger moved.